# THE STRANDED PATRIOT

*Georgia Patriots Romance: Steele Family Romance*

## CAMI CHECKETTS

*Birch River*
PUBLISHING

# COPYRIGHT

*The Stranded Patriot: Georgia Patriots Romance: Steele Family Romance*

Edited by Daniel Coleman, Janet Halling, and Jenna Roundy.

Cover art by Steven Novak Illustrations.

# FREE BOOK

Sign up for Cami's VIP newsletter and receive a free ebook copy of *The Resilient One: A Billionaire Bride Pact Romance* here.

You can also receive a free copy of *Rescued by Love: Park City Firefighter Romance* by clicking here and signing up for Cami's newsletter.

# CHAPTER ONE

Ally Heathrow darted around massive men in tailored suits and beautiful women in designer dresses, bent on finding one particular Georgia Patriots football player in the middle of this mansion full of them. Bucky Buchanan, the eccentric owner of the Patriots, had explained that as the new head of the Patriots' marketing team, Ally was to come to his party this weekend, track down one Preston Steele, wide receiver extraordinaire, and talk him into being their poster child for her social media idea. Bucky had reiterated that she couldn't force him—social media wasn't in Preston's contract—but in Bucky's words, "Gentle persuasion by a gorgeous woman isn't unethical."

Preston had been her first choice, luckily, because no one told Bucky no. He was a good old Southern boy with a whole bucketful of charm. From a marketing perspective, he was marketing gold but also a nightmare. He said and did whatever he wanted. She'd tried to tell him repeatedly he couldn't objectify her, or anyone else, as a "gorgeous woman." His compliments didn't mean much to her as she'd never been, nor would ever be, the "gorgeous woman," but he kept giving them.

She spotted Preston Steele talking to Mike Kohler next to an open patio door. The air conditioning was running on this warm early summer night, but they'd left the doors open so the party could flow from the banquet room onto the spectacular mani- cured yard and flower gardens of Bucky's estate in Marietta, Georgia.

Preston and Mike. Now that was a beautiful pair of men that would stop any woman in her tracks. She smiled to herself. Who was objectifying now? But heaven help her, it was rough not to notice. Preston had wavy, brown hair, olive-tinged skin, deep brown eyes, manly but sculpted lips, and the perfect length of facial hair. Mike had tightly curled black hair, smooth, deep brown skin, almost black eyes, and full lips. Mike was a couple inches taller than Preston's six-four. They both had perfectly sculpted muscles evident under their fitted tuxes.

She smoothed down her pale blue dress. Her naturally tanned skin was exposed by the dress's off-the-shoulder style, and she prayed the dress didn't look as painted-on as it felt. Her long dark hair was in a pile of curls on top of her head, which the makeup artist said gave full advantage to her "curvy" features. Curvy was a very kind way of putting it. She'd been downright chubby as a teenager, and though she tried hard to be healthy, thin was never a descriptor anyone had given her.

Her little sister, Kim, was a Hollywood star and was all dimples in her beautiful face and skinny but shapely. Ally's entire child- hood and teenage years had been spent helping Kim succeed.

Ally's twin sister, Shar, looked a lot like Kim, and everyone sang their praises. Ally's mom kept telling her she was a successful, talented, and driven woman, yet her parents had never once told her she was attractive. It would've been a lie, but didn't parents naturally think their children were cute? Not hers, apparently. She knew they loved her and were proud of her. It shouldn't matter that they didn't think she was pretty.

As Ally sidled in Mike and Preston's direction, she tried to decide if she could play this out like Bucky had demanded. She wanted to stride right up to Preston, tell him the idea she was already passionate about, and simply let him accept or reject it. Bucky had told her explicitly not to do that or she'd lose their one shot. He wanted her to lure Preston to the gardens, flirt with him, warm him up to her, and ease him into her scheme. The idea was laughable. Ally couldn't flirt with the likes of Preston Steele. If there was a list of most attractive and eligible bachelors in the nation, he was on it. After a few rejections from boys as a young teen, she'd put her head down and worked, using her mind, her determination, and her smart-aleck tongue to be successful at school and her career. She'd never attempted to learn the art of flirting.

Straightening her shoulders, she reminded herself that she had earned her job as head marketing manager for the Patriots, after her uncle connected her with Bucky. She was somebody, and she had a job to do. Plus she'd paid a lot of money to look as attractive as possible tonight. Now to pray that it worked.

She'd almost reached them when Preston glanced her direction and the world around her disappeared. Their gazes locked, and she was lost in the delicious indulgence of chocolate brown. His beautifully sculpted face had nothing on the power of his warm gaze. Never in her life had a man looked at her like that. Swaying on her heels, she prayed hard for inspiration. How to get him alone and beg him to help her, without falling prey to his charm or his handsome face. After Googling him constantly over the past few weeks, she'd learned that a man like Preston gave hundreds of women looks like that, women who were tall, thin models. At least he appeared interested and not repelled by her. That could work in her favor. For marketing, that was.

She tried to bat her eyelashes and give him what she hoped was a come-hither look, but she had no clue if she'd done it right. She'd only seen those kinds of looks on television, never practiced them out on anyone.

Preston didn't break away from Mike and stride purposefully her direction. Not that she was surprised. She took a few stuttering steps his way, focusing on those deep brown eyes, and ran into someone's back. The contents of his drink went flying, but luckily the liquid didn't hit anyone but the floor.

"For the sake of Pete," Ally muttered under her breath.

The man she'd smacked into turned around in surprise, but his face quickly transformed into a wide grin.

"Apologies," Ally said.

"No worries, but it seems I've lost my drink. Would you like to join me for a refill?"

"No, but thank you for being a chill cucumber about it."

He laughed. "Just one drink?"

"Maybe next time."

He held up his empty glass to her. She bowed slightly and turned away, focusing on Preston again. She could do this. She could do this. Confident woman, that was her. Confident in her hard work ethic, not her alluring smile. She was going to be sick.

Aiming what she hoped was a flirtatious smile at Preston and discreetly tilting her head toward the patio, she strutted away from the guy she'd hit and straight past Preston and Mike. She drew close enough to brush Preston's arm with hers, and she got distracted by his vanilla and sandalwood cologne. Oh, wow. Did all men smell that good? When she glanced over her shoulder, he was following her with his eyes. She tried to wink but failed as both eyes temporarily closed. Goodness' sakes that was awkward.

Easing out the side door, she was pretty sure the most desperate guy in Georgia wouldn't have gone for her weird little display. Hopefully the witnesses to her awkward flirting were few. Hopefully she could find Preston alone later tonight and march up to him without any stupid games, like she'd wanted to do all along. Why did she listen to Bucky? He was only her boss and she only loved her job.

The patio wasn't as crowded as the house, but there were still too many people for her to have the private conversation she wanted to have with Preston, if some miracle occurred and he followed her. Not knowing what else to do, she sauntered across the patio toward the flower gardens, hoping beyond hope that he'd follow her. She discreetly looked back, and her stomach hopped when she saw Preston's broad shoulders clear the doorframe. He was focused on her and moving fast her direction. Oh my goodness, it had actually worked. Yes! The makeover she'd paid for today must've been better than she thought. When she'd looked in the mirror, she'd simply seen the same rounded cheeks with a lot more makeup on, but it appeared Preston thought she was attractive enough to follow.

She debated stopping and waiting for him, but she wanted to make sure they were alone and out of earshot of anyone to have this conversation. There was also an undeniable thrill that she'd never experienced, being trailed by this powerful and handsome man. She reached the flower garden, and the heady scents of clematis, roses, and wisteria combined to make the moment feel even more mysterious and romantic.

Romantic? *Stop it, Ally*, she commanded herself. She wasn't here for romance; she was here for work, and it was guaranteed that Preston had no romantic intentions toward her. The way she'd felt when Preston met her gaze and then trailed her with his eyes was messing with her usually rational brain. She stopped underneath a canopy of trees and turned to face him.

Preston had a slight smile as he approached her. The way he filled out that tux made her stomach swirl with heat, and she clamped a hand to her abdomen. Had she ever been this close to a man this appealing? *Be calm, be professional.*

"Hello, Preston Steele," she said in a cool voice as if she had nothing riding on this conversation. Only her job, and the fabulous and charitable social media campaign that was her brainchild. Being attracted to Preston Steele could not factor in.

"Hello, Alyandra Heathrow."

"Ally," she automatically corrected. Arching an eyebrow, she found herself easing closer to him. "You know who I am?" That made more sense. He'd followed her because he was intrigued that the marketing person wanted to talk to him. Of course he didn't want to talk to her personally.

A slow grin grew on his face, making his cheek crinkle and robbing the oxygen from her lungs. Curse Preston Steele's appeal. She was not supposed to be affected by him like this. She was supposed to use his appeal to bring happiness to those going through rough times and in turn sell out the stadium, a harder feat this year with their newly inflated ticket prices.

"I know who you are." He also stepped closer, and his firm chest brushed her bare shoulder.

The suit coat buffered the impact, but Ally hadn't dated since middle school, and the contact thrilled her from her head to her painted toenails. She sucked in a breath and felt her heart thump faster.

"Head of marketing," Preston said. "The woman most of us try to avoid."

Ally blinked up at him. Avoid? Ouch. "What's that supposed to mean?"

"I'm not a rookie, Miss Heathrow. If you're giving me come-hither glances and brushing against me in a crowded ballroom, you're on a mission for Bucky. The question is, what do you and Bucky want from me?"

She'd let herself foolishly believe he'd followed her out here because he was drawn to her. *Stupid female feelings and fantasies.*

*Focus on work.* "I need you ..." She paused and tried to think how to phrase it.

"*You* need me." His voice dropped, and its husky quality sent tremors through her body.

Their gazes got tangled up and she found herself being drawn closer to him, inch by inch. She could smell his delicious cologne, and the sheer power and draw of this man made her feel feminine and desirable and beautiful. It was all so unfamiliar and thrilling. Was he truly attracted to her? She knew he dated a plethora of rail-thin women. She wasn't his type, at all.

Focus, on something other than his handsome face; and explain, without giving him a chance to walk away. She didn't need him for her; she needed him for marketing. As her body eased toward his and she stared into his deep brown eyes, she couldn't have told you her mother's maiden name, let alone what her purpose was for miraculously leading this breathtaking man out into the gardens.

When they were inches apart and she was gasping for air at the meaningful look in his eyes, praying he'd reach out to her, he murmured, "You need me personally, or you need me because you're Bucky's lackey?"

That snapped her back to reality. Of course she didn't need him personally, and even if she did, she could never hope to have a man like this interested in her. Also, she was nobody's lackey. "Can we walk?" she said, as breathy as a teenage girl.

"Sure." His eyes trailed over her, and she was going to need blood pressure medication if he didn't stop being so appealing.

She pivoted and started down the trail, plunging deeper into the thickening foliage and away from the house, cursing the heels that made her not able to move faster. For five months she'd saved up to buy these heels, hoping they'd give her confidence for parties that she'd need to attend for her job. Parties exactly like this one. Her first, and only, Christian Louboutins. Hopefully this path wouldn't damage the outrageously expensive shoes. Right now she needed distance from Preston's probing gazes and irresistible cologne. Sandalwood, vanilla, and ... was there a hint of bourbon in there? What brand was his cologne anyway?

Enough! She had to stop sniffing him and staring at him. *Concentrate, Ally.* It was time to commit him to her marketing plan and get back to work. Far away from his ... deliciousness.

# CHAPTER TWO

As Ally walked through the garden, Preston fell into step beside her, casting glances at her every so often. He was silent, and she had no clue what to say.

She was pretty sure she was messing this all up, but she'd grown up with sisters, so she didn't have a lot of experience with men to draw on. Most of her childhood and teenage years were spent following her famous sister, Kim, to different movie locations, being homeschooled or changing schools. The constant in her life had been her twin, Shar. Shar loved to tell Ally how pretty she was and Ally would laugh and say that's only because they looked like carbon copies. Yet they didn't. Shar was thin, and men clamored for her attention. Ally ignored men and focused.

She hadn't dated at all in high school, letting Kim's and Shar's adorableness take the spotlight as she focused on school. In college she'd found her spot as an academic, excelling through her bachelor and master's programs. Once she'd graduated with honors, she worked and worked until she finally arrived at her current position as head of marketing, where she could make a difference in this world. And now she was messing it all up because she wasn't attractive enough and didn't know how to flirt.

They walked quietly down a side trail, away from the lights. A pale half-moon gave them light from above, but it was a little unnerving not to be able to see through the bushes, flowers, and trees. Yet it was over-the-top romantic to be alone in this beautiful spot with a tough, manly man like Preston Steele. *Stop on the romance thoughts*, she begged herself.

"Tell me about yourself," Preston said.

"What?" She stared at his strong profile. What would he want to know about her? "About what?"

He chuckled, and the deep, husky sound rolled over her. This man wanted to know about her? "Anything." He paused as if thinking. "Where'd you go to school? What does it take to become marketing director for the Patriots?"

Work. That was familiar. She could talk about that. She cast another glance at him. Was he insightful enough to sense that work was a safe subject for her? "I went to North Carolina State for my master's in marketing. It's one of the top business schools."

"Good for you. Then you came straight to the Patriots."

She nodded. "I had a connection. My uncle knows Bucky and helped me get the job. But I worked my way up on my own."

"I'm sure you did." He smiled at her, and it wasn't an indulgent smile. It was a smile as if he actually was impressed that she'd worked her way up to her position. Now if only she could talk him into helping her.

Her heel caught on a root and she stumbled forward. Preston reached out and held on to her arm, preventing her from falling. Straightening, she pulled her arm free, humiliated that his simple touch had made her breath quicken. She was a professional, not some flighty girl, but this man was messing her up in the head.

He turned to face her on the moonlit path. His face looked softer, less intimidating but still as perfect with the pale glow from the moon. "So, Alyandra Heathrow, are you going to explain why you lured me out here?"

"Why did you follow me if you weren't interested?" she threw at him, partially biding time but also wanting to know. Lured? Could she honestly have lured a man like this? If he'd known who she was and thought she was Bucky's lackey, why did he look at her like he did and keep following her?

"Oh, I'm interested."

No! Interested? Honestly? She swayed on her heels, pretty sure she had vertigo.

His gaze traveled slowly over her, making her pant for air. His eyes landed on her lips. "So this is personal?" he asked in a husky voice.

Personal? She wanted him to repeat his past two lines in that deep, inspiring voice over and over again. He'd think she was nuts if she asked, but oh my goodness, he was incredible. Nothing about being in this garden was supposed to be personal, but it felt very personal at the moment. Preston Steele was interested in her? She wanted to do a silly cheerleader jump in the air and land in his muscular arms.

"Nothing to do with needing a marketing launch?" Preston continued with one eyebrow raised. "Because Bucky increased ticket prices and he has to fill some vacant seats of the upset fans who wouldn't make the jump."

Ally's eyes widened and she faltered back a step, reality crashing in on her. "Who told you?"

Preston's answering bark of laughter sounded too loud in the intimate space. All fell quiet again in their deserted garden spot as his stare turned cold. He leaned closer, no romantic intentions at all—but he'd probably never had any. She'd just foolishly imagined them like the inexperienced woman she was and fallen into his trap. "I should've known it was too good to be true. The most beautiful woman at this party, making a play for me with her eyes and gesturing outside."

What in the world had he just said? Most beautiful woman at this party? The words made her heart stutter for a minute, but then it restarted in a rushed but realistic beat. Preston was a womanizer. She should've known it. She'd seen all the pictures, the famous, beautiful, and thin women, but she hadn't realized he was such a player until this moment. A player and a liar.

"I'm not the most beautiful woman," she flung at him. "You're just trying to tick me off now." Upset her, confuse her, lie to her. Maybe she wasn't cut out for this job, interacting with egomaniac, flirtatious football players. Usually she could stay hidden in her office, direct projects, and accomplish work. Why had she allowed herself to get excited about working with Preston Steele?

"Complimenting you is ticking you off?" He arched an eyebrow.

Complimenting? Lying, more like it. She tried to act as if men complimented her every day. "Pretending as if I lured you here with my looks, as if men like you don't have gorgeous women coming on to them every other second."

"Men like me?"

"You know *exactly* how irresistible you are," she flung at him. Of course he did. He was probably laughing inside, knowing an overweight woman like her could never hope to date someone like perfectly-built like him. "Women flock to you, probably have since you were in diapers. It's not as if you aren't impervious to someone like me smiling at you."

He smirked at her, confirming his player status. "You're upset that I claimed you used your looks to lure me here, but you're claiming I'm a playboy with women crawling all over me?"

She stood on tiptoes and got in his face, suddenly brave and mad. He would never truly be interested in her, and she'd probably just ruined any chances of him helping her with her media campaign. "Deny it," she challenged him.

"You deny that you didn't entice me here for Bucky," he threw back at her.

How could he think she could entice any man? Least of all someone with his status and looks. She sighed. It was done. She'd officially messed this all up. Next time someone needed to interact with a hot, single team member, she'd send Juliette or one of the other pretty girls on her staff. Now she was going to have to find someone else to be their new face for social media. Someone easy. Mack Quinn and his adorable new wife would be fun. She'd seen them inside at the party. Maybe a happily married couple wasn't as intriguing as the beautiful enigma in front of her, but she could make it work. Somehow.

Turning, she gave up on the idea of Preston Steele before it even began. He caught her bare arm in his hand, and his warm palm made her flesh tingle. Did a handsome man's touch feel like that to every woman? She'd never thought of it before, but she'd have to ask one of her sisters.

She glanced up at him and tried to act civilized, leave on a good note. "It's fine, Mr. Steele. I'll inform Bucky that you aren't interested."

He stared down at her, and she felt herself being drawn back into his snare. Not a playboy? Ha. He was too good with those eyes to not be teaching classes on how to make women flock to a man. "Why don't you just ask me?" he asked softly.

"Ask you?" She had a lot of too-personal questions she wouldn't mind asking him. Did he have a girlfriend? Was he really only drawn to tall, leggy blondes like the pictures showed? What would be his idea of an ideal date? Oh my, she was being stupid.

"What it is you want." His smile this time was kind. "I know how Bucky works. He's a great guy, but his demands are not something you trifle with. What does he want you to talk me into?"

Ally hoped her answering smile wasn't wobbly. Maybe Preston really was a nice guy who would stop misleading her with smoldering looks and showering empty compliments. Maybe he would at least listen to her ideas and consider helping her and the team. "We need something that makes our social media explode," she got out.

"So of course you thought of me." He gave her a cocky grin.

Ally laughed. This fit him: overconfident and funny. Attracted to her? Not in the cards. "Of course."

Preston smiled. "What ideas do you have?"

He was interested. Ally started spouting out her idea: "I want to do a huge giveaway, one of those where you share your sad story and have to tag twenty people on social media and they tag more and it gets millions and millions of likes, tags, and shares." She'd seen it work with really desirable giveaways and huge social media presences getting behind it. This idea of hers had the power to do that. But it hinged on the man in front of her. The man who had her tied in knots, probably without meaning to. "Then we narrow it down to a hundred entries, screened for the most intriguing and touching stories, of course," she hastened to add.

"Of course." He was looking at her as if she were very interesting but very odd. That was okay. She mostly avoided looking at men close to her age, but this look was much more familiar than the intrigued looks he'd given her earlier.

She continued her explanation. "Then it gets even bigger with the news outlets getting involved. Everybody trying to figure out who will be worthy of the prize. The winner of the prize will be chosen from those one hundred screened entries by popular vote. One vote per device."

"Ally." He stopped her with one word. Her nickname. He hadn't said her nickname before, and she loved the way it rolled off his tongue.

"Y-yes?" She clasped her hands together so she didn't reach out to him. He truly was an irresistible man. Which was good ... for the media blast and the promotion. It didn't matter for her personally.

"What is the prize?"

She found her gaze riveted to his, though she wanted to look away and mumble it. "You," she finally admitted.

His gaze darkened and he tugged at his tie.

"It's just dinner."

"I see." He backed up a step, and she missed that warm cologne muddying her senses.

She stepped forward, wrapping her arm around his forearm. My, oh my, there were a lot of muscles in a simple forearm. She shook her head to clear it. "We wouldn't ask you to do anything illegal or immoral."

"Hmm. Isn't that sweet of you." He leaned in, and something in his gaze warned her to tread lightly. "So you lured me out here." He gestured around at their darkened, deserted spot of garden. Too far away to even hear the party, or risk anyone else passing by. "Flirted with me." He gave her a significant glance, and she couldn't deny that she'd given flirtation her A game—had it actually worked? "So you could use my face and my fame to bring women in who will explode social media clamoring to get a date with me? Did I miss anything?"

"Yes!" This wasn't about the women he could drag in, though it would help bring more attention to the prize. Of course the handsome bachelor's mind went there. Everything was probably about more women on his arm for this guy. "You missed a whole lot, Buster."

"Buster?"

She was fumbling. "I never said we were giving away a date with you. It's an ... opportunity to spend time with you."

"Big difference."

"It is," she shot back, pushing closer into his space. "Listen to me. When we narrow it down to one hundred entries, it will only be the sweet and adorable stories that get through. The little boy who idolizes you, the gentleman who served in the military and his only dream before he dies is to meet you and watch you play live, the teenage girl who has leukemia and thinks you're the hottest guy ever. Can't you envision it? There are so many touching stories, and the world will see and love them all. We'll feature three to four each day for the thirty days leading up to the first game of the season. Then, when the season starts, the winner will get front-row seats to the opening game and dinner with you afterwards." She hoped he was catching the vision and getting excited. She'd gotten excited every time they'd brainstormed about it. "It's for a good cause, and everyone will be thrilled that you're willing to do it."

"A good cause?" He peered down at her with his eyebrows arched. "An insane social media blast right before the season starts so we can fill the stands is now classified as 'a good cause'?"

Her cheeks and neck got hot. "I mean, not that part of it, but the stories will be touching and inspiring, and making someone's dreams come true *is* a good cause."

"Have you researched me?" he asked evenly.

"Yes." There was no reason to hide it. Where was he leading her now?

"Did you find anything about my little sister, Lottie?"

She nodded. "Lottie has Down syndrome. She's a beautiful, sweet girl."

"Yes." He was the one leaning closer now, and she really liked the smell of his cologne. She wasn't a drinker, but the smell of bourbon got her every time. "Lottie has a charity. Lottie's Loves."

"Yes," she said eagerly. "I saw that in my research but couldn't find much about what she did with it."

His expression was compassionate but belittling. "You wouldn't find much. She doesn't need or want exposure, and my parents and each of us brothers fund it. She spends her free time quietly researching with the help of some of her teenage friends, and they find emotionally-riveting stories, stories you'd probably love to feature on your social media blast." Now his look was pointed. "And they use the money in the fund, and Lottie's well-known brothers, to make dreams come true."

He was even more impressive than she'd thought.

"I've met a little boy with leukemia and his parents for dinner, after they used my front-row seats to a football game. Jex has taken a teenage girl who has a crush on him, and cystic fibrosis, flying in a paraglider. Gunner has taken an entire family who lost their Navy SEAL son on their dream trip at an all-inclusive private resort in Belize. Slade recently hired a man who was close to ending it all because he was an ex-convict and couldn't find a job to provide for his twin baby girls who were born with holes in their hearts. Do I need to keep going?"

Ally stared at him and tried to breathe throughout his tirade. Well, tirade wasn't the right word, as he'd shared it all calmly. Shame crept over her, and she didn't know what to say. Her life was marketing and media exposure. That's how her world worked. She'd never imagined someone was doing things like this but not needing fundraising money or wanting the glory or more followers on Instagram.

"You've never seen any of these stories, or a dozen more, on social media because we choose to experience them with our new friends as quietly as possible." He took a long breath and backed away from her. "I'm happy to help people and love making dreams come true, Miss Heathrow, but I refuse ..." He paused to give her a piercing stare. "To be part of a 'good cause' that is truly just a media ploy."

There was nothing she could say. He was right. He and his family were saintly, and she was focused on a different plane. She could argue that her ideas still helped people, but it was also true that her ideas were about bringing more attention to the Patriots, and selling tickets was the long-term goal. "I apologize for wasting your time, Mr. Steele."

He studied her, then finally gave her half a smile. "Don't apologize. I enjoyed it ... the luring me in, at least."

He was mocking her. She hadn't lured him in. It wasn't possible. Humiliation was her companion as she turned and started to walk away. It was obvious Preston Steele thought she was a shallow woman who used her marketing skills to expose sad stories. She was never letting Bucky push her again. Her idea was great, and she could send some of her marketing team after other players and see who wanted to get involved. Someone would see it was a charitable idea and not just selfish. Someone would like it. That player might not have the fame, looks, or charisma of Preston Steele, but it would still work. Front-row seats alone were pretty fabulous.

She heard a grunt and paused. Something thumped on the ground behind her. Whirling, Ally searched the moonlit trail but didn't see anything. "Preston?" she whispered. "Mr. Steele?" Where had he gone?

Creeping back toward where she'd left him, she saw his inert form on the ground at the same time that she heard movement through the bushes to her right. When she turned to face the threat, she gasped when three men leapt at her. A scream ripped from her throat but was cut off by a hand over her mouth. A needle plunged into her neck, sending cool liquid surging through her veins. Ally screamed again and flailed and fought, digging her fingernails into an arm, biting the hand on her mouth, but she couldn't budge any of the hands or bodies pinning her in place. Darkness overtook her, and she mercifully sank into it.

# CHAPTER THREE

Preston blinked into the darkness, but it didn't clear. His head felt foggy and achier than after his last concussion. His body was heavy and disjointed. He was lying facedown on a metal surface and quickly realized his hands and feet were bound together. Everything seemed to be rocking slightly, making him dizzy and nauseous. He could hear the thrum of an engine and smelled diesel fuel.

As the third of four brothers, you didn't call for help—it just wasn't done—but Preston had never been hog-tied and obviously drugged before. All he remembered was watching the alluring, shapely Alyandra Heathrow walk away, then taking a solid hit to the head, but he had no clue how he'd ended up here. He was terrified and confused and he let a yell of "Help!" out before he could stop himself.

"Preston?" a female voice asked from close by. He could hear the person scooting closer to him and then smelled the delicious scent of coconut. It almost negated the diesel fuel smell. Sadly, nothing could negate the unsettling situation or the pain in his head. "Preston?" she repeated. "Are you okay?"

"Who are you? What's happening?" he demanded.

"Ally Heathrow."

He tried to arch up but couldn't move. He'd thought it was Ally in here with him, but his question had meant to ask who she *really* was and what she was hiding. In the garden, Ally had claimed to have tempted him there for some social media stunt. She was beautiful and intriguing, but did she seduce him away from the party for social media, or something more nefarious? "Who are you really? You lured me into that garden so somebody could kidnap me?"

"Oh!" He heard her grunt of disgust. "As if I could lure you anywhere. I'm not involved in this. I'm tied up too!"

He wasn't sure what to believe, and his panicked mind couldn't process any reason why someone would kidnap him and Ally Heathrow. He barely knew her and he'd done nothing to tick anybody off—well, unless they were fanatical sports fans and were mad that he'd beaten their favorite football team. But come on, nobody was that crazy.

"Where are we?" Preston continued with the questions, glaring into the surrounding darkness. "Is there anyone else in here with us? Has anyone talked to you? Are you tied up?"

"I only came to a few minutes before you did. I haven't heard anyone else moving around. I was propped against the wall with my hands tied behind me."

"But not your feet?"

"No."

"Can you work your way around to my hands and we can see if we can loosen your knots or mine?"

"Sure." She scooted around, and a few seconds later her hands brushed his, sending a tingling of warmth and reassurance through him—which was insane, because there was nothing reassuring about this situation.

She started working on his knots but didn't say anything. He could hear water lapping against metal. Maybe they were on a boat? The thrum of the motor eased as if they were slowing and then the noise stopped completely, but the diesel smell lingered. He didn't like that engine stopping. Would someone come for them now?

"Sorry I accused you of being part of this," he said.

She grunted but didn't answer him.

"Do you have any clue why someone would want to kidnap you?" If he had more facts maybe he could figure out how to secure their freedom.

"Nobody would want to kidnap me," she shot back, her fingernail digging into his wrist.

"Ow."

"Sorry," she muttered. "It's you they're after. I'm just an unfortunate extra for them to deal with."

Preston felt a stronger terror rush through him at the way she'd said that. Human trafficking. He hadn't lied when he'd told Ally that she was the most beautiful woman at that party, the most beautiful woman he'd seen in a while. Some of the guys had joked about it, said how smart Bucky was to hire such a pretty, shapely marketing director, as none of them would be able to tell her no. But that beauty was now a terrifying thought, a huge bonus for a trafficker hoping to make a big paycheck off of her. She had to get his ropes free so he could protect her. Yet how many men, weapons, or debilitating drugs did their captors have at their disposal? He hadn't even seen anyone coming last night—well, he thought it was last night. They'd had little trouble incapacitating him, and could easily do it again while they had their fun with Ally.

"Any luck on the ropes?" he muttered, not wanting Ally to know what he was thinking. Then again, judging by her comment, she might have already allowed her mind to go there. A shudder passed over him.

"I think the knots are loosening. Are you cold?"

"No." He wasn't about to tell her why he'd shivered.

The door was flung open and bright light spilled in, outlining two silhouettes. Preston blinked up at them. No! The fear of what could happen to Ally overshadowed everything else. These men might hurt him physically, but he could handle that a lot easier than them hurting or exploiting Ally. He hardly knew her but felt fiercely protective of her, probably an instinct he would feel for any woman placed in this situation. Had he gotten her into this because of his fame?

The two men eased into the small room, not saying a word. Ally scrambled to her feet and stood in front of him, bravely facing them. Preston struggled to get to his knees, but the ropes were tied too tightly.

The light illuminated the small space, which looked like an empty storage closet. Two more men appeared at the door, partially blocking the light, but it was easy to see the machine guns held loosely in their hands. Preston's stomach took a nosedive.

One of the first men to enter yanked a knife out of his belt. He tried to navigate around Ally to get to Preston. Ally threw herself at the man, knocking into his other arm and luckily not spearing herself with the knife.

"Ally, no!" Preston yelled, bucking his body to try to break the ropes or somehow hit the man.

"You won't hurt him!" Ally screamed, unable to do much besides push at the guy, with her own hands bound behind her back. She was a glorious sight with determination to protect him evident in her beautiful face and the lines of her curvy body. Her dark hair was falling out of its updo and curling wildly around her face.

"Don't hurt her," Preston commanded the man. "I'll pay anything, do anything."

The other guy in the room grabbed Ally and pinned her against him. He smiled, appearing to enjoy the contact far too much.

"He cut ropes," he said. None of the other men showed any emotion to Ally's or Preston's passionate pleas, and that scared Preston almost as much as the guns they held, and the knife coming his direction.

The man knelt next to him, lifted the ropes away from his lower back, and sliced the rope that tied his ankles to his hands. He then carefully cut the ropes binding Preston's ankles, sheathed the knife in a holder on his belt, crouched, and helped Preston scramble to his feet. Preston's hands were still bound behind his back and his heart was still thumping out of control, but as the men in the doorway backed up, he breathed a little easier. They'd gone to a lot of trouble to kidnap them. Maybe all they wanted was money. He had plenty of that.

The four men marched Preston and Ally along a brightly lit, spacious hallway. Preston's head was feeling a little better but still had a dull throb. They climbed some steps and pushed out a door onto a wide deck of an obviously expensive yacht. From what he could tell, they were anchored in lots of turquoise-blue water. A small man with Spanish ancestry dressed in business casual sat at a glass patio table, typing away at a laptop.

Preston and Ally were brought to a halt a short distance away, next to some plush outdoor couches. The men stepped back, but two of them kept guns trained on Preston. The man at the table ignored all of them; Preston assumed he was trying to intimidate or belittle them.

Ally looked beautiful and terrified, still wearing her fancy pale blue dress and heels from last night. Preston wished he could squeeze her hand or comfort her somehow. He tried to communicate with his gaze that he would protect her, that she'd be okay. She focused on him and gave him a brave smile, impressing him even more. She seemed to be dealing with all of this much better than he was. He returned the smile and mouthed, *"You'll be okay."*

"No, she might not be okay, Mr. Preston Steele." The man at the table spoke and stood so quickly that Preston jumped and turned to face him. He had a distinctive Spanish accent but spoke perfect English.

The man took his time, walking close and checking them out as he came. He was almost a foot shorter than Preston's six-four; he was even shorter than Ally with her high heels on. He reeked of expensive cologne and dirty power.

"I'll pay any number you name to secure her freedom," Preston said, as evenly and dispassionately as he could manage. As nice as the yacht was, Preston was very afraid that this wasn't about money. But wasn't everything about money to a guy like this?

"No, Preston," Ally shot out. "I'm not going without you."

"Ally." Preston wished he knew her better, knew how to beg her to go if they'd set her free. He didn't think she understood the difference between what they could do to him and what they would do to her. His headache grew in force again.

The little man smiled. "Don't worry. You'll get your wish to be together."

"What do you want?" Preston ground out.

"I'm about to tell you—patience, large American football player, patience."

Him saying patience like that dug at Preston. His older brother Jex was fond of saying, "Patience, my boy, patience." He'd even said it in some of his YouTube videos. Had this guy stalked Preston's family?

"I am Carlos Sanchez the Third." He paused as if they should be impressed. When neither of them acknowledged his name, he pushed out a frustrated breath and pointed. "You see the beautiful island over there?"

Preston's and Ally's gazes swiveled. There was indeed a beautiful tropical island a few football fields away that Preston hadn't seen initially. It had some elevation and lots of lush foliage. It was probably less than a couple miles in circumference.

"It's a lovely spot. There's a natural spring that feeds a beautiful waterfall, giving fresh water and a spot to bathe." He smiled as if he was a tour guide. "There are fresh mangos, papayas, guava, and coconut. No natural predators on this exotic retreat—maybe a few spiders. Nothing that can actually kill you." He pointed to a speedboat tied up to the platform at the back of the yacht. "I have been generous enough to prepare boxes full of food and bedding for your stay. Well, enough for Preston to survive on for a few weeks. You'll have to ration with the two of you."

"You're leaving us on a deserted island?" Preston stated.

Carlos laughed. "Apparently you haven't taken too many hits to the head, football star. You guessed correctly."

"Why?" And how long would they spend here? Trapped on a tropical island with Ally didn't sound too bad, and it was infinitely more appealing than staying with these men or his fears of them trafficking Ally and torturing him, but why would this man go to all the trouble of kidnapping them just to strand them here?

The man moved quickly, getting right up in Preston's face and poking a finger in his chest. "Your brother stole my brother. When he sees that I've captured you, he'll make an exchange." He smiled again and his gaze slid to Ally. "When the boys told me how the woman came back to check on you so they decided to bring her along, I assumed that's even better insurance. Maybe your brother doesn't love you as much as I love my brother, but he's a former American military hero. Of course he would want to rescue the pretty lady."

Ally flinched at his words, and her dark eyes narrowed.

"Gunner stole your brother?" Preston was confused and suddenly sick. He'd blamed Ally for luring him to the spot where they were captured. How wrong he'd been. It was his fault Ally was in this mess.

She was still glaring angrily at Carlos, but then she met Preston's gaze, and the vulnerability in her eyes made him want to protect her even more. She didn't say anything, standing stoically and bravely in the face of these men who were most likely either terrorists, drug dealers, traffickers, or all of the above.

Carlos nodded grimly. "And I want him back."

"But if Gunner stole your brother ..." Preston's mind was whirling. "He would've taken him for the United States Navy. They're not going to negotiate with you." If Gunner couldn't negotiate with this man, would they just leave Preston and Ally here until they died? Send them to Gunner piece by piece until they got what they wanted? What if Preston had just said the wrong thing, making this man realize how stupid his plan was, and they'd simply slit their throats and drop them in the ocean?

The man barked out a laugh and stepped back, spreading his hands. "Your brother does not work for the United States military."

"Excuse me? Gunner's been in the Navy since he graduated high school." Gunner had always been more serious than the other brothers and had enlisted in the Navy, gone to the Naval Academy, then trained as a SEAL. From all they'd heard, he was highly decorated; his most recent rank advancement had been from lieutenant to lieutenant commander. Their mama was very proud and spent a lot of time on her knees praying.

Smiling silkily, Carlos shook his head. "Your brother has been lying to you. He hasn't been in the Navy for almost a year. He is currently one of Sutton Smith's operatives. Do you know of Sutton Smith?"

Preston nodded, wondering why Gunner or this man would lie to him. "I met him at a party last year." He'd been impressed with the distinguished man and his famous wife, formerly a duchess and named the most beautiful woman in the world. Preston glanced at Ally again. He'd told her she was the most beautiful woman at that party last night. It was still true, but their sickening situation made looks pretty unimportant. He wished now that she wasn't so tempting so the men around them wouldn't be inclined to go after her.

Carlos chuckled. "You Americans and your stuffy parties." He gestured to the two of them. "Enjoying a fancy party at the illustrious Bucky Buchanan's mansion when my men disabled the security sensors, cut through a back fence, and took you. Bucky loves his beautiful ladies." He leered at Ally's chest. "Too bad he doesn't spend as much effort protecting their lovely bodies."

Preston's stomach churned at the way Carlos was staring at Ally. He'd rather be stuck on that island for years than allow Carlos to touch her. His gaze darted to the four armed men. He'd go down fighting if any of them attempted anything. Maybe it was stupid, but he was a Steele and could never allow a woman to be injured while he sat by. Gunner was the noblest of any of them. Could he truly be lying to their family? Why? They all would've understood if he retired from the Navy and worked for the illustrious Sutton Smith.

"Look at you." Carlos's gaze swept over Ally, undressing her with his eyes. "All dressed up and so incredibly beautiful, but I'm sure you've never been to a party like I would host." He eased in closer to her, and Preston tensed. "Would you like to come to one of my parties? We can dump Mr. Steele on the island, and you ..." He licked his lips. "You I would spoil rotten."

"No, thank you," Ally said with plenty of spice and bite in her voice. She tilted her chin in an obvious challenge. "I'd rather swim with the sharks."

Carlos looked startled at her rebuff. Preston inched closer to them; thankfully, the guards' attention was on Ally as well, and none of them swung their gun to bear on him. His hands tied up, no weapon, and five to one. The odds weren't great.

Carlos chuckled and then tsked. He ran his tongue over his lips and his eyes swept over her fitted blue dress again. "It's a pity. Such a body. Wasting away in the hot sun. Maybe dying here if

Gunner Steele doesn't return my brother in full health. Are you sure you wouldn't rather come with me? I would never force you to do anything, simply let you enjoy my spacious estate in Colombia and give you time to see that I'm worthy of your affection."

Preston was almost in the right position. He could tackle the first gunman into the second one, and maybe in the confusion he could maneuver the knife off one of the men's belts and cut his ropes free. Then he could grab one of their weapons and have a fighting chance. He didn't think they wanted him or Ally dead, so that would work in his favor.

"I truly appreciate the offer," Ally said. Preston saw the flicker of disgust in her eyes and respected the bite in her voice, though he hoped it didn't make Carlos furious. "But I'm pretty partial to Preston, the hot sun, and remote tropical islands."

Carlos studied her for a few seconds. Preston's heart was thumping uncontrollably at the crazy move he was about to pull. He was ready to leap when Carlos clapped his hands together and smiled. "Well, my dear, don't say I didn't offer when you're sticky with sweat, bored with Preston's company, and sick of spiders crawling over you." He laughed. "Let's get you two to your tropical paradise. You'll be able to grow really close until your brother comes for you."

Preston's brain didn't catch up as quickly as his ears. Carlos wasn't going to force Ally to stay with him or attack her? He was going to send them to the island unharmed? Relaxing his taut stance, he didn't question Carlos's decision as two men grabbed him and two took Ally's arms and walked them to the speedboat.

"Best wishes," Carlos called from the yacht as the men cast the ropes off from the yacht and started the motor. They pulled away from the yacht and toward the island.

Preston glanced back at Carlos again. Carlos was watching them go, and his eyes were cunning, but Preston was too relieved that he hadn't touched Ally inappropriately to worry too much about that look.

# CHAPTER FOUR

The boat cruised through calm waters and toward the island. The men with them stayed stoic and silent. Preston wished his hands were free so he could hold Ally and reassure her. She was handling all of this so bravely. Did she truly want to be with him, or was that just a line to keep Carlos away? Most likely just a line. She didn't even know him very well.

She was staring at the island but must've felt his gaze. Turning to him, she blinked quickly, looked down at the floor of the speed-boat, and then away again, but not before Preston saw a tear crest her thick lashes and roll down her smooth cheek. She'd been so brave, and obviously didn't want even him to see any sign of weakness, but she had every right to cry. Most people would have dissolved in a puddle of tears long before this. It made him feel guilty that she was crying and he could do nothing to help her.

The boat eased into a small bay and one of the men stowed his weapon and jumped out into the waist-deep water, holding the boat in place. It hit Preston that he had no clue if they were in the Caribbean, Micronesia, Somoa, Fiji, the Maldives, the Philippines, or hundreds of other options. A suffocating feeling pressed down on him as he saw miles of blue ocean surrounding them, no boat, except Carlos' yacht, or land on the horizon. If Carlos never told anyone where they were, they truly might live out their lives here. Never to see his family again. Never to play football. Never to find love and marry. Never to eat another hamburger. He shook these thoughts away. There would be time to freak out later. Right now, he needed to keep protecting Ally.

One of the men next to Preston unsheathed his knife again, and Ally gasped. Preston wished he could get closer to her and reassure her. Not that he was feeling too calm or untroubled himself, but he felt driven to protect her.

"To cut our hands free." Preston said the statement calmly as if he could guide their intentions. "Right?"

The man simply looked at Preston as if the words meant nothing to him and kept moving toward Ally. Her eyes widened and she shrank against the man holding her. Preston's palms grew clammy and his heart raced. They wouldn't go to all this trouble just to slit their throats now.

"Don't hurt her," Preston commanded.

The man gave him a perturbed glare and kept advancing on Ally. What was going on? Why wouldn't they respond to him?

Preston yanked himself away from the man holding him. He didn't know what he could do with his hands bound, but he wasn't going to stand by as they cut Ally.

The man with the knife whirled on him, surprise in his dark eyes. The man who had been holding Preston dove for him. Preston elbowed him and scrambled toward Ally.

The man who had jumped into the water leapt back into the boat and yelled, "Stop!" He pounced on Preston, and the men's combined weight knocked him to the fiberglass floor of the boat.

"Preston!" Ally screamed.

Her scream tore at him, and Preston struggled to free himself from the weight pushing him down. He'd been in many a wrestling match or fight with one or more brothers, but never with his hands tied behind his back. It was impossible to really fight without your hands free. Preston bucked his body and tried to thrash and kick, getting in one good headbutt.

"To cut ropes, to cut ropes!" the man yelled in his ear.

Preston stopped fighting. "You won't hurt her?" he asked.

The man sighed. "No. Our job to cut ropes. They no speak the English."

Preston finally realized why the men were so quiet. It had taken a while to reach that conclusion, but he could blame it on his throbbing head or all the drugs that were probably in his body. More likely it was the stressful, insane situation they were in, and his mind was trying to find a way to protect Ally and understand whatever Gunner had done.

"You no fight more?" the man on top of him asked.

"I won't fight anymore, if you promise not to hurt her."

"We don't hurt her," the man said.

Preston felt like he could finally breathe. He probably shouldn't trust the man, but he didn't have a lot of choice. "I won't fight," he said.

The men lifted off of him, and Preston struggled to his knees, then pushed up to his feet. He focused on Ally. Her lower lip trembled, but she didn't say anything or break down into tears. Man, she was brave and impressive. He wouldn't have blamed her for throwing a fit or dissolving into sobs. He was tempted to do both himself.

"Loco Americano," one of them muttered.

The other two nodded, not smiling or laughing.

Preston felt worse than loco. He felt off-balance, groggy, in pain, and uncertain how he and Ally were going to deal with being stranded on this island. Yet he'd rather be stranded than around these men any longer, wondering if one of them would go after Ally at any moment.

He restrained himself as the man went toward Ally again with the knife. "It's okay," he reassured her, though nothing felt okay at the moment. The sun was bearing down on him, making him sweaty, and he had the insane thought that he wished he'd been kidnapped in anything other than a tuxedo.

Ally focused on Preston, and he gave her what he hoped was an encouraging smile. She flinched as the man walked around behind her with the knife, but she stood stoically brave. The man sliced her hands free. She pulled her hands around and rubbed at her wrists; they were red, but she looked okay.

Relief rushed through Preston. The man had done what they'd said.

The guy with the knife walked to him next, and Preston held his hands out away from his back. The knife cut through the ropes easily and Preston shook his arms out, rubbing at his wrists also. His shoulders relaxed, though his neck was still tight and his head aching. He nodded his thanks to the man.

"You get off boat," the man who could speak English instructed.

"Gladly," Preston muttered.

He walked toward Ally, took her arm, and helped her over the side of the boat, plunging in the waist-deep water next to her. Wrapping his arm around her waist, he slogged through the salt water with her up to the beach. His shoes and suit pants were soggy and filled with water and sand.

He bent low and whispered against Ally's cheek. "You okay?"

She glanced up at him, her dark eyes somber. "I'm not sure," she murmured.

He could understand that. Stopping on the dry sand, he turned back to the men, who were carrying boxes off the speedboat. At least Carlos was true to his word and was leaving them with supplies. How long would the supplies last, though? How long would they be here? Gunner had taken Carlos's brother, so obviously the man was a criminal of some sort. Would Sutton Smith or the government, if they'd already turned the criminal over, allow them to make a trade? Would Carlos even give Gunner their location, or would he let them waste away?

The men carried the two boxes up to the edge of the sand where some palm trees shaded the spot. The island was lush and beautiful. It would be a dream come true for a vacation, but the thought of being stranded here, with no one but criminals knowing where they were, made it into a definite nightmare.

Preston guided Ally with his arm, moving through the sand. She stopped, bent forward, and unstrapped her heels. Preston noticed the men watching her with far too much interest, as the movement revealed her neckline and her shapely legs. Did she have any clue how appealing she was? The sooner he could get the men to leave, the better. Straightening, she held her shoes in one hand and gave Preston a forced smile.

Soon, they reached the shade of the palm trees. The sand was harder packed in the shade where the men had left their boxes of supplies.

The man who spoke English turned to them and pulled out a phone. He held it up and gestured to them. "I take picture to show brother you here."

Preston nodded and wrapped his arm around Ally. Turning her more toward the trees, he hoped some of the background showed in the picture. Maybe there was no difference between tropical islands in different regions, but he hoped there was, a specific tree or ... a snake hanging from the tree. He gritted his teeth as he saw the snake coil and slither up the branch. He hated snakes. Pushing the slimy feeling of snakes away, he thought about Gunner. His brother was more serious than the rest of them, and Preston knew Gunner would do everything he could to find them.

Neither of them smiled as the man took several pictures with his phone. He pocketed it, leered at Ally one more time, and raised a hand to them as the other men strode back to the boat. "Good wishes."

"Thanks," Preston grunted.

The men pushed off, started the boat, and motored back to the yacht. Preston stood close to Ally, watching them go. Ally still seemed in control. If not for the slight trembling he felt from her pressing against him, he wouldn't know she was upset.

He studied the yacht out in the ocean, only blue for miles and miles around it. It was good that Ally was in control, because he was having a meltdown inside.

# CHAPTER FIVE

Ally was going to dissolve into a puddle of tears at any moment. The only thing holding her up was Preston's arm around her. The air felt sticky and oppressive around her as she watched the yacht motor off into the teal blue ocean. The ocean of nothingness. Everywhere her eyes darted, there was nothing but blue.

She pulled in a quick breath, but she couldn't get enough oxygen. Realizing she was leaning heavily into Preston, she tried to push away, but she felt too weak to support her own body weight. Maybe it was whatever drugs they'd knocked them out with. Maybe it was the heat and the lack of water. Maybe it was the oppressive fear that was sucking the hope, faith, and happiness out of her.

Squeezing her eyes shut, she prayed silently for help and strength.

"Are you okay?" Preston bent down closer to her.

He was a big guy, strong and tall, and she appreciated how he'd tried to defend her around those men. Those men could've easily taken advantage of her. That slimy Carlos who kept giving her empty compliments. So gross. Bile clawed at her throat at the very thought of one of them touching her. She said another prayer of gratitude that they were gone. Being stranded was horrific, but anything was better than staying with their kidnappers.

Awkwardness crept over her, and she didn't answer him immediately. No matter how tired and afraid she was, she needed to be strong. She sidestepped away from him and straightened her shoulders. "Thirsty," she managed to get out.

Preston studied her. He seemed to be the quintessential gentleman and protector of women, as evidenced by how he'd reacted to shield her from those men, but she didn't like being in a vulnerable position with a well-built man she didn't know. She didn't know enough about men to know how one would react in a situation like this. Would Preston go into "me Tarzan, you Jane" mode? The only reassuring thing was that she wasn't Preston's type. Yet would that matter if she was the only option and he was used to women clamoring over his perfect body at all times?

"Me too," he said, rather than comment on her keeping her distance. "Let's go find that fresh water Carlos promised." He grimaced as he said it, probably thinking exactly what she was thinking: How did they trust anything Carlos said? For all they knew, this island was overrun with modern-day pirates or poisonous scorpions.

The hyperventilation returned. "Shouldn't we ... I don't know, start a signal fire with the rum?" she tried to joke, referencing *Pirates of the Caribbean*.

Preston laughed. "Good idea. Let me see if we've got any." He winked at her, and the air grew hotter.

He bent down and opened the closest box. Ally couldn't resist easing in closer to see what was in the box. All she could see was boxes of granola bars and crackers and some cans of food.

He held up a can opener and a vicious-looking knife. "Well, at least they thought of a couple things we'll need."

As he opened the next box and shuffled through it, Ally could see what looked like either a tent or a hammock. She was praying for a tent. She hated spiders and would struggle sleeping thinking about them—and what if there were snakes? She shivered. Snakes.

There was a small box that said "inflatable pad" and a bag that contained a fleece blanket. It was hot enough she didn't like the thought of a blanket, especially a fleece one, but maybe they'd need it. Preston lifted up a towel, a little toiletry kit, and then a huge gray T-shirt and some large, soft-looking cotton shorts. There was more food in the bottom.

"No matches?" she asked.

Preston grunted in disgust. "Nothing to start a fire with." He squatted next to the boxes and shuffled through them both again.

Ally glanced at the thick greenery. Who knew what was in there? Ugly creatures, ugly pirates? She gave herself a shake; freaking herself out would do nothing. "Do you know how to get a spark with a stick, or something like that?"

Preston shook his head. "They left that one out when I was a Boy Scout. Flint and steel wool was the craziest we got." He dusted his hands off and stood. "I guess we wait on the fire."

"Okay." She studied the boxes at their feet, not too keen on staying in this dress until Preston's brother came. "That's all the clothing in there?"

"I'm afraid so." Preston shrugged out of his suit coat. If she was hot, he had to be sweltering in that thing. Despite her worry of being alone on this island with a man she didn't know, it was impossible to not notice how perfectly Preston filled out his button-down shirt.

He looked her over, and Ally tilted her chin defiantly. She must look like a mess, but what did that matter right now? She'd taught herself not to care what a man thought of her looks; only her brain and hard work mattered. "What?"

"Like Carlos said earlier, they didn't plan on you being with me." Preston lifted his shoulders and pointed to the supplies. "One-man tent, one towel, one sleeping pad, the ... lack of clothes for you."

Ally pulled in a slow breath, wanting to scream at him that it was his fault she was here, but compassion swelled in her—he looked as if he were beating himself up. "If they wouldn't have brought me, think how miserable you'd be alone."

Preston's eyes widened. He shoved a hand through his hair. "I really appreciate the kindness behind that statement, but I'm calling myself all kinds of names inside. The question is ... why aren't you calling me names?"

Ally stared at him. "It's somehow your fault that your brother captured Carlos's brother, a man who is obviously a criminal, and Carlos retaliated on you and me?"

His shoulders lowered and his dark eyes got warmer. "I had no idea you were this ... amazing."

Ally shook her head. "What are you talking about?"

Preston stepped closer to her. She held her ground. "Some of the other players have made comments about how ... curvy you are and how they hoped the head of marketing got a hold of them and stuff like that. I've been intrigued by you, and of course I noticed how beautiful you are, but I had no idea you were also chill and nonjudgmental."

Ally's chest warmed at the compliments and her dry mouth got even dryer. Preston was an extremely handsome man—and from all appearances, he was a good man—and they were stuck alone on this island, possibly until they died. Did he really think she was beautiful? The other players saying she was curvy didn't matter to her; it was just another way to say overweight. Preston's compliments made her wonder if she could trust him or if he was just a schmoozer who said what he thought a woman wanted to hear. She'd never heard someone say she was attractive, not that she'd ever asked.

"So if a woman is ... beautiful—" She cringed at that word. "—they can't also be 'chill and nonjudgmental'?"

Preston smiled. "Don't twist my words. My mom is absolutely

classy and beautiful but still chill and nonjudgmental." His face crumpled as if someone had jabbed him with a knife.

"What's wrong?" Ally stepped closer and touched his arm. "Are you okay?"

"My mom," he murmured. Looking away, he shook his head. "This is going to kill her."

Ally thought of her own parents, her two sisters. How upset and concerned they would be. Her youngest sister, Kim, had recently reunited with the love of her life, and their wedding was in four days. "I'm going to miss Kim's wedding," she said.

"Your sister?"

She nodded tightly.

"Ah ... I'm sorry. I'm sure they'll postpone it, until we're rescued."

She didn't know what to say. She was sorry too. They'd only planned on enough food for him, for—what had the guy said, several weeks? She was going to go insane here for that long, if they didn't die of heat exhaustion and lack of fresh water first. How close was the water? Was there even a spring on the island or had Carlos lied to them?

They stood there for a few beats. The beach was silent aside from the soft lapping of the ocean. Maybe they were in the Caribbean, as calm as the waves were.

"We can't do this," Preston declared.

Ally focused on him. "I don't see that we have much choice."

"No. I know we have to do this." He smiled and pointed around at the island. "But we can't let ourselves wallow and get depressed. Let's go explore, find where we want to set up camp. We'll build shelters and maybe even a boat, find fresh fruit, start a signal fire with sticks, kill fish and snakes and ..."

Ally's stomach plunged as his voice trailed off. "Snakes?" she squeaked out.

"Um ..." Preston forced a smile. "I mean, if there are snakes. Maybe lizards or crabs or scorpions."

"Stop!" Ally held up a hand, trying to stave off her horror. "You aren't making this any better. Have you seen snakes or scorpions?" Preston lying and claiming that she was attractive to him was the least of her concerns. She was stuck on a deserted island with spiders, snakes, and scorpions?

Preston shook his head quickly. "I'm just saying, whatever creature might be on this island that we don't like—" He held up the knife. "—I'll kill it. That'll make us feel better, right?"

Ally grunted. "I'd rather pray there are no vicious creatures on this island. Carlos said only spiders." She shivered.

"See? You don't like spiders." Preston grinned like a little boy with his first pocketknife. "I'll kill them."

"What is it with you and killing?" She put her hands on her hips.

He smiled impishly, finally looking chagrined. "I grew up with brothers, right on the coastline south of Boston. We explored, we built forts, and we killed dangerous creatures. It's a boy thing."

She rolled her eyes. "I only had sisters."

"Ah, that explains it."

"What?"

"The aversion to killing dangerous creatures. We aren't going to kill the fluffy bunny rabbits or endangered turtles."

Her eyebrows popped up. "Well, thank heavens for that. You're like a little boy trapped in a buff man's body."

He grinned. "I'm feeling immensely better. This will be like being a Boy Scout again—exploring, building things, killing stuff."

"Stop with the killing. Please."

Preston shrugged, and she had to admit he was growing on her. He was easy on the eyes, but he also had an infectious mischievous spirit about him. "All right. But you'll let me kill the spiders?"

"Yes. I won't complain if you kill spiders or ... other scary things." She shuddered, not wanting to think about what might be in this jungle. "Let's go find water now."

"Good plan." He nodded, but instead of walking into the thick greenery in front of them, he bent down and scooped up her Christian Louboutin silver heels, which she'd taken off to get through the sand earlier and then dropped by their supplies. She hoped they weren't ruined from the salt water. That was admittedly the least of her concerns, but she'd still saved up over two thousand dollars to buy them, hoping they'd give her confidence for big parties like the one last night at Bucky's. Such parties, and the job she'd worked so hard for, seemed a lifetime away on this beautiful, but unsettling spot of earth.

Preston dangled one shoe by the strap over his finger; it looked small and delicate next to how tough and big he was. He held the other shoe against a tree trunk and lopped off the heel with his knife.

Ally gasped like someone had punched her in the gut. Her beautiful shoes. "Wh-what are you *doing?*"

"Sorry." Preston didn't sound nearly repentant enough for butchering her beautiful shoes. She'd said he could kill spiders, not her favorite, most expensive item of clothing. He exchanged the first shoe with the second, and as a scream worked its way too slowly up and out of her throat, he chopped off the other heel.

"No!" she screamed, staring in shock at her massacred heels. The distinctive red sole had a gaping wound with the absence of the heel. "Those were Christian Louboutins!"

He held the knife loosely in his right hand and her mangled shoes in the other. "Now they're practical."

"What?" she gurgled out.

He smiled sheepishly and extended the shoes to her. She gingerly grasped them, not wanting to feel the gaps where the heels used to be. Glancing down, she saw the three-inch heels on the ground amidst leaves, sand, and sticks. The red was splashy, like blood, against the natural greens and browns. Her shoes!

"Didn't you ever see *Romancing the Stone?* My little sister, Lottie, loves chick flicks, so we've seen every one my mom cleared as sweet enough for her. She's really ... innocent."

Ally just kept on staring at him. What did chick flicks have to do with her shoes? It was interesting that this tough man in front of her had a tender side and would watch chick flicks for his sister, but why had he killed her shoes, then?

"In the show, they get stranded somewhere in the jungle like ... I think Columbia, maybe. Anyway, she's wearing heels, and he cuts off the heel and she freaks, like you just did." He smiled as if she were cute or something. "And she says all shrilly, 'Those were ...' some fancy brand, and he says, 'Well, now they're practical.'"

Ally clung to her shoes. "Practical for what? We're stranded on a deserted island!"

"But we still have to walk through that to find fresh water and a more protected place to shelter." He pointed at the dense foliage. "I didn't want you navigating it barefoot or in heels."

Ally could see the practicality of that, but ... "Couldn't you have asked me?"

"Would you have said yes?"

She rolled her eyes. No, she wouldn't have been able to part with these heels. The thought was ridiculous, since they were probably ruined anyway, and ... she didn't want to think about the fact that they may never get back to civilization. He was right: she didn't want to be walking around barefoot or in high heels.

Bending forward, she started to strap the mutilated shoes on, her too-tight party dress riding up on her legs and down in the front. Preston cleared his throat. She glanced up at him, and the way he was looking at her made her even hotter than the tropical sun. "What?"

"You should be careful doing that move." He sort of growled low in his throat. "The way those men looked at you when you did it earlier ... it made me want to fight them all."

Ally straightened and stared at him. Her putting her shoes on was some sexy, tempting move? How could she be sure he didn't turn into a caveman when she had no clue how men worked?

When she said nothing, he glanced away and cleared his throat. "We probably should change before you put those on." He loosened his tie and pulled it off, dropping it next to one of the boxes. Then he started unbuttoning his dress shirt.

Her mouth went dry. "Change?" She looked away, studying the waves gently rolling onto the soft sand. "What am I going to change into? There are no clothes here for me." It was sickening to think that she was the add-on. If she hadn't lured Preston out into Bucky's garden last night, or whenever that party was, she wouldn't be here. Those men must've been watching him and just waiting for the perfect opportunity to grab him and when she'd turned back to check on him, they'd gone after her too. Yet she hated the thought of Preston being here alone. That was dumb, as she hardly knew him, but she'd felt very protective of him when that man had pulled the knife in the yacht and she'd stepped in front of him to try to keep the criminals from spearing him.

She heard Preston's shirt drop, and her breath stuck in her lungs. She couldn't even bring herself to look at him when he didn't have a shirt on. How was she going to spend who knew how long stuck on this island with him? Looking everywhere but at him, she waited for the answer to her question.

His footsteps approached, and she studied his long legs, still clad in his wet dress pants. Preston reached out and gently tilted her chin up with his fingers. Ally should've closed her eyes, but she didn't. Instead she let them trail up his body, taking in his toned abdomen and defined pec muscles. Her eyes brushed over his well-built arms and shoulders; then she finally met his gaze.

His eyes were filled with humor. "I take it you've never seen a man without a shirt on."

Ally gulped and shook her head, dislodging his hand. "No. I mean, at the beach and stuff, but I didn't have brothers, okay?" This had nothing to do with siblings. If she looked at a brother the way she'd just studied Preston, that would be all kinds of disgusting. Preston was ... not disgusting. Very appealing. Very manly. Very tough. How in the world was she going to be alone with him? He should put that extra large T-shirt she'd seen in the box on. Right now.

"I'm sorry to embarrass you. I think it's great how pure you are. But we're going to be alone on this island for ... a while. Are you going to be okay seeing me without a shirt on?"

"Put that stupid T-shirt on!" she almost screeched at him. No, she wouldn't be okay. Why would he insist on not wearing the T-shirt? He'd get sunburned or bug bites, or she might just touch him to see what that taut skin felt like, and that would make things awkward between them. She knew he couldn't truly be interested in her, and she wanted to keep her distance, keep herself physically safe from a man, but also emotionally safe. As inexperienced as she was at dating, she could easily fall hard for a man like Preston.

"The T-shirt is for you," he said softly.

"Me? It'd be huge on me."

"It'd be like an oversized T-shirt dress. My little sister wears them all the time, and Slade recently bought a bunch of them for his fiancée, Mae. She loves T-shirts." He smiled. "With funny sayings on them."

"Are you overexplaining everything because you're nervous?"

He nodded. "How would you feel if you were constantly staring at the most beautiful woman and knew you were stranded with her for the immediate future?"

Ally gulped. He couldn't possibly mean that. "The most beautiful woman on this island?" she challenged, folding her arms across her chest to protect herself from his silky smooth tongue.

"That's not what I said at all."

"Stop with the compliments, please."

His brow wrinkled.

She wanted to play it off that she was a professional woman, not the type who wanted to hear that she was beautiful. The truth was that she had rarely heard it, unless a man was trying to get something from her, and she certainly didn't believe it coming from an enigma like Preston Steele.

"I apologize," he said stiffly.

"It's fine." It wasn't fine that he threw empty compliments

around like sand, and she had no clue how to deal with him, but she could adapt. She'd spent her life working hard and adapting to be successful.

Preston offered her the shirt, dispelling her awkwardness. "Will you wear it? It'll be much more comfortable than your dress."

Ally looked down at her tight formal dress. At this point, it felt like it was sewn to her body. She'd love to change. Taking the shirt, she said, "Thank you."

He met her gaze. His dark eyes were incredible, with dark lashes and brows. His short facial hair framed his appealing lips. With his fame, athletic prowess, and looks, he had to beat beautiful women off with a stick. He was probably just used to women throwing themselves at him and was waiting for her to do the same. Why did he keep claiming that she was so beautiful? She'd bet he threw out empty compliments so often he didn't even realize he was doing it.

"Of course," he said.

He didn't say anything about her not taking his compliment, or about her being uncomfortable seeing his chest. Which she appreciated, because she was definitely not comfortable staring at his well-formed muscles.

She motioned with her hand. "Turn around so I can change."

A slow grin grew on his face. "So I guess we're not going to get cozy with minimal clothing on around each other."

"No! And you'd better know right now that I'm a good Christian girl, and you're going to keep your hands to yourself while we're stranded here."

His grin stayed in place, and instead of looking upset, he said in a husky voice, "That's why you're so appealing."

"Excuse me?"

"Women who are pure and beautiful. It's the most attractive combination in the world."

Ally's breath rushed out at his words. She really needed a drink of water, some shade, his eyes to stop drinking in her face, to get away from here. She inhaled deeply and forced herself to say, "Can you go up into the trees or something for privacy?"

"I don't want to let you out of my sight until we know what's on this island." He pushed a hand through his hair. "I don't really trust Carlos's word that we're safe here."

"Good point. Please turn around, then."

He nodded. "Would you turn as well? I'll change into the shorts."

Man, it was hot and sticky on this island. Her stomach was so full of heat and longing she could hardly stand it. What was he doing to her? All he'd asked was for her to turn her back, but the thought of it ... Whew! These feelings were unfamiliar, unsettling, and yet amazing to her. She whirled quickly, setting the shirt on a tree limb so she could unzip her dress.

Hearing his sharp intake of breath, she stopped mid-zip. "Are you looking?" she demanded.

"No," Preston said with a low grunt. "But I still have ears."

"Well, plug them."

He chuckled. "I promise not to turn around. It's just ... rough being this intimate with you."

"Well, we're not going to be intimate," she said primly, "so stop implying it."

A few beats passed with her afraid to unzip her dress or even move. He didn't say anything. She wanted to whirl around and see what he was doing, make sure he was facing away, but that wouldn't be good. She wanted to try to trust him.

"You know what I mean," he said in a deep, sonorous voice. "The entire situation is intimate. I won't try anything, I promise."

She couldn't handle it. She whirled around. He was facing away from her, true to his word. His dress pants were still on, and he cut a beautiful, irresistible figure with his broad back popping with muscle.

"You won't touch me?" she asked, breathlessly.

"Are you facing me?" he asked.

"Yes."

He turned back around, slowly. Ally was able to appreciate every glorious inch of him. How hard had he worked to form a body that incredible? Professional athlete. It was his job, right?

"I'm going to have to touch you, Ally," he said patiently, as if she were a three-year-old. "The tent is small, and it's safer if we both sleep in it."

Ally was panting for air again. She hadn't even considered the tent. How was she going to protect herself from falling for him? The few times he'd touched her, she'd liked it—too much. Oh, heaven help her know how to deal with a man. It was a foreign problem to her.

"I'll need to touch you to keep you safe. But ..." His face fell. "I won't kiss you or touch you unnecessarily ... unless you want me to."

Kiss her? Want him to? Every part of her wanted him to, and she barely knew him. It was safer to focus on the misery of being stranded and never eating chocolate again than it was to think about him kissing or touching her. Wow, he was direct, and she was ... falling for him.

No, that was nuts. They were stuck in an extreme situation. It was natural they would lean on each other and physically have to touch, but she was driven, focused on her career, and she didn't need or want a man in her life. Especially not a man who would eventually make her feel like less. When, or if, she did settle down, it would be with a studious, serious man like her father. Not some burly, handsome football player. Preston wanted to kill things with a knife, for heaven's sake.

"Thank you," she said briskly. Then she shooed him with her hand. "Now turn around and get changed. I want to find a drink of water."

He laughed and spun again. Ally let herself study his broad back for a second, but when he unzipped his pants, she whirled to face away, her cheeks and neck flushed with heat. She said a desperate prayer: *Please bless there are no deadly animals on this island, I can keep my hands off that beautiful man, and we can find water and have enough food. But most of all, please, please let Preston's brother find us soon.*

# CHAPTER SIX

Preston knew there was a lot to worry about with survival and being stranded on an island: food, water, dangerous creatures, no way to make a signal fire, Carlos and his men coming back, and Gunner possibly never finding them. He knew those should be his primary concerns right now, but he found his thoughts consumed with the witty woman he was stranded with. He loved her purity and the light that shone from her eyes. She reminded him of his little sister, Lottie, who was an angel. But he had no sisterly feelings for Ally. He'd never been so attracted to a woman. She was very different from the bony models he usually dated, and he loved her curves and soft, smooth skin.

"Okay, you can turn around now," she said.

He smiled. He loved how she'd been obviously affected by seeing his chest. Many women chased him simply because he was a Patriots football player or a Steele brother or they thought he was good-looking. So many brazen women had hit on him in the most obnoxious ways. Ally had acted shocked and enthralled with his chest, as if she'd never seen a man without a shirt on before. She also seemed embarrassed or almost upset when he complimented her, as if men weren't fawning over her all the time, and she was innocent and unspoiled. He liked her a lot.

Turning, he glanced over the much-too-big T-shirt on her. The neck hung down, revealing her smooth neck and the appealing length of her collarbone. The sleeves covered her upper arms, hanging past her elbows. The body was shapeless and much too big—drowned her was the only way he could think to describe it —but he loved the way it made her look so feminine. The best part of all was her shapely legs poking out underneath the shirt, as it stopped a few inches above her knees.

"It looks ... pretty awful," she said.

"What?" How could she think that, and how could a woman as beautiful as Ally ever doubt that she was attractive? "No." He stepped up closer to her, awed by the way he was drawn to her. He'd dated many famous women who had absolutely no effect on him while they were professionally dolled up, yet Ally in a huge T-shirt could literally make his knees weak. "You look ..." Irresistible, gorgeous, sexy? None of those would work and help him keep his attraction to her under control. "Really cute."

She blinked up at him, as if she doubted his words. Her eyes trailed over his shoulders and chest. "You look ... huge and tough."

He laughed. "I spend a lot of hours in the gym. Professional duty."

"It's a mighty fine look on you." She quickly glanced away.

Preston's eyebrows arched. She didn't appear to be any more comfortable giving compliments than she was receiving them. Bending down, she started strapping on the heels that weren't heels anymore. Preston had to look away as the T-shirt rode down on her neck, giving him a glimpse of a silky undergarment. He needed to be a gentleman, or he would be in trouble. He'd told her earlier how upset he'd been when she'd done that same move with her shoes and those men had leered at her. She hadn't responded. Maybe he was scaring her because he was so attracted to her. He'd promised to stay in control, and he would, no matter how tempting she was.

As she straightened, he smiled gently at her. "We're quite the pair. Me in cotton shorts and dress shoes, you in a massive T-shirt and heels."

"Not heels anymore. You killed them, remember?"

He chuckled. "I do remember. Sorry about that."

"Ha! You realize when somebody says 'sorry about that,' they basically mean 'I couldn't care less.'"

"That's not true. I didn't mean it like that at all." He said it in a low voice, as he didn't want to push the point. She seemed to finally be relaxing around him, much to his relief.

She arched a challenging eyebrow. "Let's go find water. I'm so thirsty."

"Okay." He was thirsty too, hot and sticky. He hoped there really was safe water to drink, or they'd be in trouble and quick. "Speaking of killing, though ..." He bent and swept up the knife, transferring it to his left hand.

"No more talking about killing." She gestured. "Lead the way."

He nodded and took a few steps into the dense foliage, but then he stopped. "I just thought of a better idea."

"What's that?"

"I wonder if we shouldn't walk the perimeter of the island. If there's really a waterfall, there should be a stream coming out to the ocean. It would be much easier to follow a stream to its source than fight through this." He pointed at the thick greenery.

"Okay. But what do you mean, 'if there's really a waterfall'? There had better be fresh water, or I'm tracking that Carlos guy down."

He smiled at how cute and feisty she was. They fell into step side by side, staying at the edge of the forest. The heat was oppressive, even in the partial shade, and sweat trickled down Preston's back.

"Are you comfortable like that?" she asked him after they'd walked in silence for a few minutes.

"Like what?"

"Shirtless." She didn't meet his gaze, and Preston thought again how much he appreciated her innocence.

He shrugged. "As an athlete and one of four boys, I've lived a lot of my life without a shirt on. It's a lot nicer without a shirt right now, not as hot. I was dying in that dress shirt and slacks."

"I bet."

They walked along, silently working their way along the curve of the beach. He must've misjudged the size of the island. If it was less than two miles around, like he'd assumed initially, they should've walked the entire perimeter, but he hadn't seen any stream and they weren't back to their boxes of supplies. They had no choice but to keep moving and hopefully find water. Preston was used to extreme workouts, sometimes without water in the heat, so he was doing okay.

Ally looked like she was fading. She swayed and fell against a tree, scratching her arm on the bark. "Ouch," she muttered so quietly he barely caught it. She definitely wasn't a dramatic type of girl.

Preston stepped in close and inspected the scratch. It was red, but the skin luckily hadn't broken. He hadn't seen any medical supplies and hated the thought of one of them getting hurt out here. It was possible there was someone else on the island, but he doubted it. Carlos wouldn't have left them any help, unless it was someone intent on hurting them. He'd already lied saying there were only spiders, and Preston had seen that snake. He shuddered.

Wrapping his arm around her waist, he said, "Lean on me. I'm sure we'll find water soon."

Ally did lean into him. "Sorry. I'm not usually the wussy girl, but I'm so thirsty I'm getting dizzy."

"You're doing great. We'll find the stream soon," he repeated as they shuffled forward. If they got back to their starting point and the supplies without finding a stream or water source, they'd have to plunge into the interior and fight their way through the thick greenery.

"Why aren't you dying like I am?"

Preston smiled. "I'm used to working out in the heat. Do you like to work out?"

"Ha," she grunted out. "I enjoy running, but my mom's always harped on me about the idiocy of it."

"Excuse me?"

She straightened, not leaning on him so much. "I'm ... out of it right now. Forget whatever I say. I do like to walk or jog, in the mornings, with plenty of water."

"That's why you look so good."

Her body felt stiff against him, and he feared he'd made her uncomfortable. He loved her curvy shape, but couldn't understand why her mom had "harped on her about the idiocy of running."

He didn't feel comfortable prying, so he said, "What's your favorite spot to run?"

She talked slowly, as if she were drained. "Well, downtown I like Freedom Park. In Buckhead, near my parents' house, I loved Tanyard Creek Park."

A creek sounded nice about now. "How far do you usually run?"

She glanced up at him. "Jog," she emphasized. "I'm not an ultra athlete like you. I'm happy to do a few miles."

"I never run distance," he admitted. "Sprints, but never more than an eight hundred, so a few miles sounds impressive to me."

"Thanks."

They shuffled along, and Preston wanted to know more about her. A lot more. He liked how chill and uncomplaining she was, that she was successful at her career, and he also liked how she often phrased things in a funny way.

"Preston!" she screamed.

He jumped. "What?"

"A stream." She pointed, and his eyes followed her finger. Around the bend up ahead, a trickle of water came down out of the jungle and made its way to the ocean, carving a small creek bed through the sandy beach. "Thank heavens," she breathed. Pulling away from his arm, she hurried to the stream. Preston followed. She dropped down to the water and dipped her fingers in, then gave him a brilliant smile. "It's cool."

"Cool as in cold, or as in 'this is so cool, we finally found fresh water'?" He grinned and knelt next to her.

She giggled and splashed some at him. "Cool as in semi-cold."

The water felt great. He dipped his hands and splashed it on his face.

"Do we dare drink it?" she asked.

"Probably smarter to drink closer to the source. I hate the thought of you getting sick."

She cocked a gaze at him. He was struck again by how beautiful she was. Her features were soft and feminine, her dark eyes sparkling and appealing, and her skin was smooth and a deep tan. "Only me?" she said. "You don't care if you get sick?"

He laughed. "I'm not thrilled about the idea, but I'd take a fall for you."

She looked shaken. Glancing away quickly, she sprang to her feet, suddenly invigorated. "Let's go find the source, then. I'm thirsty as a horse after racing the derby."

He let her lead the way as they trekked along the edge of the small creek. It cut through the jungle pretty effectively. Occasionally, she'd lift a branch out of the way and he'd hold it for her as they both went through. Her makeshift flats couldn't be too comfortable to walk in, but she didn't complain. Preston was getting blisters in his dress shoes, but he wouldn't say anything.

The splashing of water grew louder as they progressed through the jungle at a slight incline. Preston's eyes darted around, but he didn't see any creatures that were threatening. He'd gripped the knife the entire walk and wished he had a sheath for it. These shorts fit fine, but they weren't tight or thick enough for him to dare put a knife through the waistband.

A small clearing opened up ahead, and Preston could see a shallow pool of water and a trickling waterfall spilling into it from about ten feet above. He wondered how long it had been since it had rained here. Hopefully the water was clean, or they'd be in a lot of trouble. The clearing was shaded with trees and had a decently level spot where they could put their tent.

"Can I drink now?" Ally asked eagerly.

"I think it'll be okay."

She did that incredibly sexy move where she bent down and slid off her strappy shoes, the shirt riding up on her legs. His mouth went dry, but he couldn't find the willpower to look away. She smiled up at him. The longer they were together, the more relaxed she seemed around him, and the more he reminded himself he couldn't relax around her.

Straightening, she left her shoes and waded into the pool. The pool was clear and clean-looking, the bottom rocky. Ally slipped and slid around in the knee-deep pool, looking so irresistible in that ridiculously huge T-shirt. He about suggested she take it off so she didn't get her only comfortable item of clothing wet, but he wasn't sure how that would be received. And the thought of her in only her underwear was enough to make more sweat drip down his back.

She reached the waterfall and stuck her hands under it, cupping the water and drinking. Preston was really thirsty, but he could've stood there and watched her all day.

"Are you coming?" she asked him.

He nodded dumbly and slipped off his shoes and socks, then eased into the water. The coolness felt great on his raw heels, but the rocks, though they were smooth, were uneven and dug into the soles of his feet. He made his way across the small pool and to her side. She glanced up at him, all cute and mischievous, and threw some water in his face.

Preston blinked it out of his eyes, smiled, and said, "You realize I grew up with brothers and we take teasing to another level."

She leaned away. "Sorry. Forget I splashed you."

"I won't forget." He winked, then cupped his hands and drank from the falls. It tasted good and fresh. Once he'd drunk his fill, he put his head under the stream, groaning with relief as the cool liquid soothed his lingering headache. They'd found water, and it felt amazing. He pulled back, blinking water from his eyes, and saw that Ally was watching him. He shook his head like a wet dog, splattering her with droplets.

She cried out, "Hey!" Then she giggled. "Guess I deserved that."

"For sure. You'd better watch your back."

She laughed again. "Sisters can be as vicious as brothers."

He lifted his eyebrows. "We'll see."

They stood there smiling at each other for a few seconds. He pushed away the worries over being stranded with no way to start a fire, her being uncomfortable with him, and not finding fresh water. The last two worries seemed to have resolved. He hoped. As long as Ally stayed comfortable around him and this water didn't make them sick.

Ally took a few more drinks, then slogged back through the water and sat on a boulder at the edge. The T-shirt rode up on her legs. She glanced around at the sparkling waterfall and all the greenery. "It's beautiful," she said.

Preston nodded. He plodded over toward her, sitting right in the water next to her. He'd worried about her getting her T-shirt wet, but found he didn't care if he was wet. He'd dry in this heat, and the cool water felt great. The only drawback was the pool was only knee-deep. If it was deeper, he'd be back-floating. "So are you," he said.

"Excuse me?" She finally met his gaze.

"You're beautiful, Ally. Much more beautiful than this scenery." When she didn't respond besides narrowing her eyes, he added, "To me, at least."

She stood quickly and edged away from him. Not meeting his eyes, she murmured, "Please don't, Preston."

"Don't ... compliment you?" He glanced up at her. She looked uneasy and he didn't want that, but he needed to know what was so wrong about him complimenting her. "Why?"

She licked her lips and studied the waterfall. "We aren't going to have some fling because we're stuck alone together."

His eyebrows rose at that. He wasn't looking for a fling, but he was sincerely interested in her and thought she was incredible—brave, funny, smart, not a complainer, the list could go on.

"You don't need to compliment just because it's what you'd do with other women."

Preston was confused. He stood in the water and asked, "Do you think I'm a player?"

She harrumphed and walked back to her shoes, bending down to strap them on. When she spoke, her eyes were fixed on the ground. "Do you want to carry the supplies up here to set up camp, then?"

"No."

"No?" She glanced up at him, tendrils of dark hair curled around her face. Most of it was still piled on her head.

"No, you're not going to dodge my question. Why do you think I'm some player who hands out empty compliments?"

She straightened and rolled her eyes. "I have Google, Preston." She frowned. "Or at least I used to have Google."

"I'm not a player," he insisted. "I date, but I don't burn through women or treat them poorly."

She folded her arms across her chest and glared at him. "Fine, you're not a player. Please stop complimenting me." Turning, she started back down the edge of the creek.

Preston scrambled over to slide into his shoes without any socks. His blisters were going to get worse, but all he cared about right now was catching up and getting a straight answer out of her. He caught her quickly and wrapped his arm around her waist, tugging her to a stop.

Ally whirled on him, her dark eyes full of fire. "Don't compliment me, and don't grab me."

The words hit him like a punch in the gut. Preston released her and stepped back, staring down at her. "Ally." His voice dropped low. "Did a man ... hurt you?"

Ally stared at him. For half of a terrifying moment, he was afraid that he'd hit the nail on the head. She was apprehensive around him because a man had hurt her. How could he convince her he'd never do the same? His size alone could intimidate a woman.

"I would never, Ally. I promise, you don't know me, but—"

"A man didn't hurt me," she interrupted him.

"Then why do you seem so ..." How did he describe it without offending her further? "Apprehensive around me?"

Ally looked down at the stream. Finally, she muttered, "I'm not used to being around men, but nobody hurt me, at least not like you're implying. Let's just set up camp and forget I said anything."

"Ally, we might be alone here forev— a long time," he amended quickly. "I want you to be comfortable around me."

Her lips twisted. "Then stop complimenting me and touching me unnecessarily. You want trust, you need to earn it." With that, she turned and hurried down toward the beach.

Wow. She claimed a man hadn't hurt her, but what did she mean, "at least not like you're implying"? Maybe a man had hurt her emotionally. Either she was dealing with some really huge issues, or she didn't like him for some reason. He pushed out a breath and followed her. Either way, he had time to figure it out. He hoped it wasn't years.

# CHAPTER SEVEN

They slowly made their way back to the waterfall. They'd completed the circle around the perimeter of the island and found their supplies not too far away. Preston had insisted on hauling both boxes. She'd tried to protest but it did no good. He was big enough that he could easily handle two boxes stacked in his arms.

Ally wished she could explain it better to Preston. He really seemed worried that someone had hurt her. She'd been hurt emotionally, but hadn't everyone? She couldn't forget seeing all those pictures of him online with thin, gorgeous women. Worse, when he complimented her, she found it harder to trust him. It made her think he was one of those schmoozers who threw out compliments they didn't mean to try to manipulate or influence someone else. Maybe it was just her lack of experience with men and her fear of being alone with an unreal attractive man. Forever. He'd almost said they'd be stuck here forever. He might not be wrong. Their food might run out, and either they'd learn how to fish and find fruit, or they'd die.

She followed his broad back along the side of the creek. Staring at his wide shoulders, which tapered down to his taut waist, she was amazed at the striations of muscle on his back. He was beautifully formed—that was for sure. He probably thought she was intimidated by his size, but she'd seen the sincerity in his eyes earlier. He wouldn't hurt her physically, and hopefully, after her sharp words, he'd stop complimenting her. When neither of them was acting weird, she enjoyed talking to him and teasing with him. Who knew that men could be so fun to tease?

They reached the clearing by the waterfall, and he set the boxes down closer to the trees, next to the little rise about fifteen feet away from the water.

"Are you worried they'll get wet?" she asked.

"If it rains, the pool might flood."

She nodded and set to work, helping him set up the small tent on the flattest spot they could find, inflate the thin mattress, and spread out the blanket. They left the towel and toiletries in the box. Looking at that tent made her apprehensive. It was probably midday, so they wouldn't sleep for several hours, but how in the world would they fit in there—together?

Pushing it from her mind, she slipped her shoes off, waded into the pool, and took a long drink from the waterfall, splashing some on her neck and face. She tried to rub under her eyes, wondering how horrific she looked with all the makeup caked on her face.

Preston's footfalls splashed through the water, and she glanced at him. He stepped up close, and her heart thudded loudly in her chest. When he reached toward her face, all of the muscles in his shoulder flexed. "You have some black stuff ..."

"The makeup from the party," she said, itching for him to touch her ... which made no sense, as she knew she couldn't let herself fall for him, and she felt embarrassed she'd been so sharp with him about not complimenting her or touching her unnecessarily.

"Do you want me to get it off?"

"Yes, please." She stood, almost afraid to move and dislodge this connection arching between them.

He ran his fingertips under the water and then gently rubbed the top of her cheek. His mouth twisted in concentration and he rewet his fingers to try again. "Stubborn stuff," he muttered.

She laughed uneasily. His touch was doing funny things to her insides.

Finally, he rubbed one last time, then declared, "I think I got it all."

"Thank you."

She thought he'd drop his hand, but instead he trailed his fingers along her cheek and across her jaw. His hand traced back into her hair as he studied her. His fingers must've hit a hairpin, because he slowly slid one out. The sensation was incredible, and Ally's body flushed with heat at the even warmer look in his eyes.

"Do you want me to pull them out?" he asked softly.

Ally should've said she could do it herself. Instead, she nodded. "Please."

He lifted both hands and tenderly worked his fingertips along her scalp. When he found a pin, he would slowly pull it out. More and more of her hair tumbled around her face, and his left palm was full of bobby pins. He cradled her head gently with his right hand. The moment went slow and sticky between them, much hotter than the tropical heat.

"You're incredibly beautiful, Ally," he murmured. His dark eyes caressed her face, as if he truly meant his words.

Who was she kidding? She stepped back and cleared her throat, awkward and unsettled and still wishing he was touching her face and looking at her in that special way. This was Preston Steele. She needed to wake up and face reality. Yet maybe this was their reality. Maybe his brother would never find them.

"Do you want me to take those?" She opened her hand to take the pins.

He dropped them into her palm and muttered, "I'm sorry." He jammed a hand through his hair, and the way the muscles flexed in his arm made her stomach flip-flop. "I forgot quickly that you don't like compliments."

"I ..." What woman didn't like compliments? She couldn't explain that she would like them if she thought they were true, if she thought he meant them. Yet that look in his eyes ... Could Preston Steele really think chubby Alyandra Heathrow was beautiful? She pushed out a breath. No. It was just this crazy situation. Yet if memory served her right, he'd said she was beautiful back at Bucky's party, but then she'd had so much makeup caked on her face he probably couldn't even see the real her.

"You're fine," she finally muttered.

The splashing waterfall was their only accompaniment for a few seconds; then Preston cleared his throat and asked, "Are you doing okay?"

"Surviving." She smiled to show him she was teasing and hopefully break the tension.

He chuckled. "That might be our MO for a while."

The beautiful yet awkward moment from before had passed. He took a long drink and then stepped under the water and let it splash over his head and face. It dripped down his chest. Ally stared like a teenage girl with a desperate crush. She couldn't have torn her eyes away if a rescue helicopter hovered overhead.

Preston's chest, shoulders, abdomen, arms ... they were all beautifully muscled, covered with smooth, dark skin, and quite simply he was glorious. His handsome face was wet from the waterfall, and with the kind way he treated her and how she enjoyed talking and teasing with him, she found herself panting for air and having delicious fantasies of trailing her fingers along his chest. Listening to him say how beautiful she was and living in a fantasy where they actually had a relationship. She hadn't kissed a boy since middle school and had never been around a man to equal this one.

Preston stepped out of the stream and blinked the water from his eyes. Meeting her gaze, his dark eyes flashed with a mixture of concern and intrigue that quickly turned to ... desire. Did he truly desire her?

"Ally?" he said in a deep, appealing voice.

Terror rushed through her. She couldn't let herself fall for him, only to have her heart broken when they returned to civilization.

Her concentration on him broke and she stumbled back in the knee-deep water, needing to get away so she could get in control of this ... attraction was the only word she could think of. Incredible attraction that she didn't need to be feeling. She could lie to herself and say it was only because of their extreme situation, but she knew no other man could or would yank her in like this. She could remember a few men in college trying to talk with her, but she'd remained focused on studying and working and they'd left her alone quickly.

Preston's hand wrapped around her elbow, probably to steady her, but it was too much contact. Heat crept through her, and it took all of her self-control not to reach out and touch him. Just one touch. That might be enough.

"Are you okay?" he asked again.

"Fine, fine. Why do you ask?" She pried her eyes from his handsome face and studied the rocks that formed their small waterfall.

"You were looking at me like ..." His voice dropped. "Like a woman looks at a man that she's interested in."

Ally's heart slammed against her chest. His words were far too bold, and they challenged her to do something about the attraction building inside of her. That would be insane. She wasn't the type of woman Preston Steele dated. No matter how kind or complimentary he was being, as soon as they returned to the real world, he'd drop her like a hot rock. If they ever returned to the real world. Many voices in her head were begging her to take advantage of this opportunity with this incredible man and just kiss him. She'd never kissed a man of Preston's caliber and never would again. Why not enjoy that he seemed willing because they were in such a crazy situation?

No! Horror rolled through her. She would be the one taking advantage of the situation if she pushed herself on him.

Pulling her arm from his grasp, she worked her way through the shallow water, the uneven rocks pushing against her tender feet. Her feet needed to toughen up. Her heart needed to toughen up more. How was she going to survive emotionally with Preston? She said a silent prayer for bravery, for protection from Preston's charms, and—most of all—for Preston's brother to find them quick.

As she walked toward the supplies, she could hear Preston coming behind her. No privacy. She was not going to have a moment alone in this forsaken paradise.

She set her bobby pins next to the small kit that had a tooth-brush, toothpaste, a comb, shampoo, body wash, and lotion, and then spun on him. His dark eyes were filled with determination, and that scared her. He was going to get to the bottom of her longing look; she could feel it. A man didn't get to Preston's level of excellence without hard work and determination. She needed to get away, and now.

"I need to use the restroom," she blurted out. It was true, but she'd been holding it so she wouldn't make things awkward.

He nodded. "Okay. I'll turn my back."

"I'm going into the trees a little bit."

"No. I'll turn my back," was all he said. He turned and faced the waterfall to give her some privacy.

Ally glared at his broad back. She wasn't going to pee right here close to their supplies, fresh water, and sleeping spot. She crept backward into the trees, hoping he couldn't hear when a branch snapped. She squatted down and peed, having to drip-dry, which was gross, but she didn't dare use a leaf without a clue what was poisonous or not.

As she straightened, she heard a sliding noise coming from her left. Her eyes darted to the sound, and her stomach dropped when she saw a large snake slithering toward her.

Maybe she should've frozen or played dead, but no way was she lying down. She shrieked and sprinted away from that monstrous terror.

"Ally!" Preston whirled and rushed toward her across the small clearing.

"Snake!" she yelled.

Preston reached her, lifted her off the ground, and swung her away from the snake. Glancing around his arm, she saw it slithering toward them. She screamed in horror. Preston pushed her farther behind him, darted to their boxes of supplies, and grabbed the knife. Ally's gut churned as she saw the snake was almost upon them. Its ugly head reared up, hissing so that its small, pointed teeth were visible.

Preston dodged the snake's head, and before Ally could do more than back into their supplies, he brought the knife down in a swift chopping motion. The knife cut most of the way through the snake's ugly body. The snake's teeth snapped at Preston's leg.

"Preston!"

He leapt away from the snake's head and plunged the knife through the body again and again. Within seconds, he'd chopped the horrific creature in half. Ally's eyes bugged out. The snake's head wilted to the ground. Preston shifted the knife to his left hand and bent down. He grabbed one end of the snake and hurled it into the forest, then did the same with the other end.

When he turned to her, he looked glorious, like a superhero. His face and body were taut and hard, ready to take on twenty more snakes. He'd just killed that snake for her.

His face softened. "Ally?" he murmured. "Are you okay?"

"Y-yes," she managed to get out.

Preston rushed across the space between them, dropped the knife to the ground, and gathered her into his arms. Ally gasped from the surprise and sheer pleasure of being held tightly against him. Her hands were balled into fists, her entire body felt coiled from the encounter, but she found herself relaxing, melting into Preston.

"It's gone," he said. "You're okay. I've got you."

Ally wrapped her arms tightly around his back and just held on.

She never wanted to leave the circle of his embrace again. Preston was safety. Preston could protect her. She buried her head in the warm flesh of his chest and prayed that was the only snake on this island, even though that wasn't likely.

He simply held her close for a while and then said, as if she was the most important thing in the world to him, "It didn't hurt you?"

"No." She quivered.

He ran his hands along her back. "When did you see it?"

"I-I stood up and the snake—it was huge! Right as I stood up, it was coming toward me. I screamed and ran. Then you killed it, like Rambo! Now ... you're holding me." She loved being held by him. It was a sense of home she wasn't familiar with, as her family had relocated so often. How could Preston's arms be home? She was probably just overreacting because of the snake. She shivered, despite the warm temperature. "Do you think there are any more?" She spoke into the crook of his neck, then let herself glance up at his handsome face.

"I don't know, sweetheart." He said the words so tenderly, then brushed some hair away from her face, and she found herself aching for him to trail those fingers across her lips. "I wish I had a clue if it was poisonous or not, and I'm afraid there are more," he reluctantly admitted.

His words slammed her back to reality—the reality that a snake could be coiling around their ankles as she was distracted by this wonderful man. She broke away from his arms and her eyes darted around the clearing, searching, searching.

Preston touched her hand. "It's okay. You're safe."

She shook her head quickly, trying to clear it. "You're right. It's okay. I'm okay. You're good at killing things with that knife. You're a good Boy Scout—no, you're like Rambo or something. I'm glad you learned to kill things as a boy." She never thought she'd be happy about killing. "And we have a tent. Snakes can't get through the tent." She looked at the tent, which looked pretty flimsy at the moment.

"I hope not." He didn't make light of her fears, instead reassuring her. She appreciated it, and she didn't care if he wasn't being completely truthful. "If another one comes, I'll kill it with the knife."

"Yes!" she said. "You will. Thank you, Preston, for being a killer." That made him chuckle. "It's all good. I'm okay, I'm okay," she repeated a few times to reassure herself. She wrung her hands together and shivered. "You have no clue how much I despise snakes."

Preston smiled grimly. "Me too."

"How did we get in this nightmare?" she muttered, staring at him.

Preston pushed a hand through his hair. "It's my fault. You wouldn't be here without me."

"Let's not go there." Now she was the one trying to reassure him. "I'm not blaming you."

Preston stepped right up to her and pushed his chest out. "Come on. I'm blaming myself. You said it. We're in a nightmare, and you never would have gotten here without me and whatever

Gunner has done." He paused. "Hit me."

"Excuse me?" She stepped back.

"Hit me. It'll help you conquer the fear of the snakes, get out the frustration over our situation. It helps, I promise." He gave her an irresistible grin. "I told you I grew up with three brothers. We hit each other all the time."

She stared at him. She wouldn't mind hugging him again, but she wasn't going to hit him. "I'm not just going to hit you."

"Try it." He offered his chest. "Use me for a punching bag. Come on. It's great therapy."

"I guess since there isn't a licensed therapist around to talk through our concerns, we'll just hit people instead." She shook her head. "You've lost it, my friend."

"Come on, Ally. You've dealt with all of this so impressively, but almost too bravely. The snake is the first thing that's snapped you. Thanking me for being a killer." He chuckled. "Hit me. It'll make us both feel better."

She glared at him for a few seconds. "You're being ludicrous."

"I know. But try it." He pushed out his chest again. He looked so good standing there, she didn't want to hit him.

"I'm hungry," she said. "Let's sort through the food."

"After you hit me."

Hit him? Maybe she'd do it once, simply to appease him so they could move on and eat something. She batted at his chest. The muscles were solid. She really wanted to open her hand and flatten her palm against those glorious muscles.

"That wasn't a punch," he said.

"Now you're just taunting me."

He grinned.

"Do all those muscles help you take hits on the field better?" They'd helped him kill that vicious snake.

He flexed, and her eyes widened. Wow. "Yeah." He eased in closer to her. "And I can take anything you can throw at me. Come on."

"What does that mean?" she asked.

He shrugged. "Tiny little thing like you, you can't hurt me."

It was the wrong thing to say—or, if he wanted to rile her up, it was exactly the right thing. Ally wasn't tiny and had never been. The way he'd phrased it made her embarrassment heat up to fury. She didn't think Preston would ridicule her for her size, but she didn't know him that well. Maybe brothers teased differently than sisters.

Winding up, she punched him hard in the abdomen. It stung her hand, but it did feel good to hit him.

"That's right." His grin grew. "Let it all out. Don't worry, you're too little to hurt me."

Ally's jaw dropped. Preston wasn't the type to mock her, but the teasing hit too close to her insecurities. She smacked him again and again. Preston hardly flinched as she landed punch after punch on his chest and abdomen. Anger overtook her as it didn't even seem to hurt him. She balled her fists, moved in closer, and simply banged on his chest. Tears sprang up and trickled from her eyes. All the frustration and fear over being kidnapped, being stranded, and seeing that awful snake poured out as she wailed on him. Past angers surfaced as well—her parents never once telling her she was attractive; Trevor Ollie pretending to like her, then telling everyone she was too fat and how gross it felt to touch her; and getting the charity invite to prom because the kid's best friend wanted to take her twin, Shar. She'd been so excited and he hadn't even asked her to dance all night, standing awkwardly by her side as everyone danced around them.

The punches kept landing and Preston kept taking them as tears raced down her face. She probably looked unglued with her hair wild and sweat popping out on her forehead.

More frustration from years past poured out. Overhearing her mom telling her dad that she was concerned about how over-weight Ally was, especially compared to her perfectly thin sisters. Being at one of Kim's movie sets, where the director wanted Shar to be part of the show, but turned his nose up at Ally. It felt like she was always comparing herself to the gorgeous Kim and Shar, yet hating herself for it. They were both kind and good and loved her, and she had this deep-seated resentment over something none of them could control. She'd semi-starved herself for years and exercised most days of the week, and though she'd lost weight and had tried to embrace her curvy body, she still wasn't fit or gorgeous like her sisters. She'd convinced herself it didn't matter, but it still hurt.

She had no clue how long she'd banged on Preston's chest and cried, but suddenly he held on to her wrists and murmured, "It's okay, sweetheart. It's okay."

She melted against him as hot tears still stung her eyes and raced down her face.

"I've got you. You're going to be okay." He released her wrists and wrapped his arms around her back.

Ally's arms wound around his waist, and she simply laid her head against his lovely chest and clung to him. Neither of them said anything as they held on to each other.

After several wonderful moments, hot embarrassment flushed through her cheeks. She leaned back and stared up at him. "I'm sorry. I went a little berserk there."

He chuckled and released one of his hands from her back to gently lift a tear off her face. "Don't be sorry. I forced you to do it. Do you feel better?"

She took a deep breath and admitted, "Yes. Who knew punching somebody could be therapy?"

"I did." He gave her a cocky grin. "But it's more the release. You were able to cry and let some of it go."

She was humiliated that she'd hit him for so long and cried so hard, but he seemed happy with the outcome. If Preston was sincere, he was the most nonjudgmental person she'd ever encountered, and the most amazing and impressive man on the planet.

"Thank you," she murmured. She pulled away and said brightly, "Food?"

"Sounds good." He gestured for her to go ahead, and she walked toward the food boxes in front of him. She couldn't stop herself from looking at the blood left by the snake, and her eyes darted around searching for more of the horrible creatures, but she did feel immensely better.

# CHAPTER EIGHT

They sat with their backs propped against a tree and ate some dry crackers and jerky, then worked their way through a can of peaches. The whole time, Preston watched Ally carefully.

She seemed calmer, and something had changed in the air between them. He was still leery about telling her how beautiful she was, even with more smears of black makeup from her crying earlier. He'd thought he'd washed all that black stuff off. At least she appeared to be more comfortable around him and trust him. Holding her in his arms had been heaven. She was soft and womanly and felt perfect cradled against him. He wondered why he'd wasted his time dating scrawny models who were all bone and hard, fake curves. Ally's shape was so much more appealing to him.

She closed her eyes and groaned. "If it wasn't so hot, I'd crawl in that tent and take a nap."

"You could take a nap right here," he suggested. Did he dare suggest she rest against him? He loved holding her close and hoped she felt the same, but he had to remind himself to stay in control and that he couldn't kiss her until she asked him to. That was a stupid agreement on his part.

Her eyes opened wide. "I wouldn't dare. What if there is another snake out there?"

Preston didn't dare tell her he'd noticed several different species of snakes. Maybe he'd reacted too violently by hacking the snake in two, but it had been a good release from not being able to fight Carlos and his men and feeling so helpless stranded here. At least that one snake wouldn't be bothering them.

"So now we have nothing to do but sit here ..." She let her voice trail off.

Sit here. For how long? He loved being around Ally, but he felt claustrophobic and scratchy at the thought of being on this island for too long. He wasn't used to inactivity. Maybe he could chop down trees with his knife and expand their shelter. Their spot had plenty of shade, but the trees wouldn't protect them much if it stormed. Maybe he could figure out how to start fire with sticks or hike around and kill snakes. That sounded like a worthy quest.

She arched an eyebrow at him. "Maybe you should tell me stories."

"About what?"

Thinking for a second, she said, "Tell me about your sister."

"Lottie." He smiled as he thought about her, but then a pang went through him. What if he never heard her giggle again, never got a tight squeeze as only Lottie could give?

He swallowed and met Ally's gaze, hoping his eyes weren't bright. Her dark eyes were full of compassion, as if she could see straight through him and understood his fears. He talked quickly, before thoughts of never seeing their loved ones could start either of them down the road of despair.

"Lottie's an angel," he said. "She's sixteen, almost ten years younger than Gunner, the youngest of my brothers. She was born with Down syndrome. My mom has worked extremely hard to help her be high-functioning—teaching her how to interact socially, be confident when uninformed teenagers tease her, how to run her charity, and to read."

Ally nodded encouragingly, so he kept going with his monologue. "She loves to read romance. We love to tease her about it. You should see how she gets all fiery and then she giggles. She's beautiful, and my mom makes sure she always has the clothes that fit right so she feels confident and attractive." He smiled. "Lottie knows exactly how beautiful she is, and she's not afraid to tell anybody."

Something flickered in Ally's eyes, something uneasy, but she simply said, "You love her a lot."

"Oh, yeah. She softens all of us crazy brothers, who like to kill things." He winked, and she gave him a full smile. "She's pretty much my favorite person on the planet."

"What do you like to do together?"

"She loves the water, so we take her sailing or swimming often.

She also loves chick flicks." He studied Ally's deep brown eyes. Most of her makeup was gone now, and she looked even more attractive to him. "Do you like chick flicks?"

"Of course. My sisters and I used to always see the newest ones together." She turned wistful again, but then she quickly said, "What are Lottie's favorites?"

"She's luckily not that picky." He smirked. "All of us brothers take turns vetoing ones that are just too cheesy. But my mom is the one that vetoes the most because of ..." He paused, realizing where he was going with this train of conversation. Ally had seemed uncomfortable with him until just recently; he didn't want to somehow mess that up again.

"Why does she veto them?"

"Well, you know, if they're too ... intimate."

Ally smiled softly at him. "That was pretty cute."

"What?" His neck felt hotter than this tropical heat could make it.

"The big tough and famous athlete who not only goes to chick flicks with his little sister, but gets embarrassed if there's a sex scene in the show."

Okay, maybe he was the one being awkward now. "Yeah, we get pretty crazy if there's a bad scene. Have you seen *I Feel Pretty*?"

She nodded. "One of my favorites."

"Really. Why?"

Ally looked away. "Just a relatable story for ... a lot of women."

Preston thought back over the story line. "So you think a lot of women are too hard on themselves and don't understand that they're beautiful in their own way?" Maybe he shouldn't have phrased it like that, but he felt bad for women who thought they had to fit a certain mold, and he didn't like the way Ally couldn't accept his compliments.

"Waxing philosophical now," she said, but the darkening of her cheeks betrayed that she was uncomfortable with the subject.

Preston didn't push it, but he wanted to reassure her she was absolutely beautiful to him—inside and out. "If we stay here very long, we'll solve the world's problems. Right?"

"Right." She laughed. "Now what were you going to tell me about *I Feel Pretty?*"

"Oh, yeah. So my mom tries to keep Lottie safe from certain scenes, but Lottie's friends had seen *I Feel Pretty,* and she'd heard all about it and begged and begged. So my mom made Slade and I promise to not let her see anything she shouldn't. You should've seen us in the theater during the ... intimate scene. I had my hand over Lottie's eyes, Slade had his hand over her mouth because she was screaming to 'let her watch,' and we both were trying to control an innocent sixteen-year-old girl who just wanted to see her movie."

"Oh my, I can just see it. That's hilarious. Poor Lottie. Let her watch her show." She winked. "I'm just kidding. It's very honorable that you want to keep her innocent."

"Thanks." He shuffled his feet through the dirt; they'd both given up on shoes pretty quickly. He missed seeing Ally put her shoes on. He glanced at her; she looked tired. "Why don't you close your eyes for a few minutes?" Did he dare suggest she lean against him?

"No way! What if another snake comes? I'd be like a little mouse just curled up and waiting for the snake to sink its venom into me."

Preston smiled. The way she phrased things was so funny, and she was dealing with this situation better than any woman he'd ever met could've. Being stranded on an island wasn't ideal, but he couldn't complain about being here with Ally.

# CHAPTER NINE

It had been one of the longest days of Ally's life. She couldn't believe that only this morning they'd woken on the yacht and then been stranded on the island. As soon as the sun buried itself in the trees, she started dropping not-too-subtle hints that she'd like to get settled in the tent—partly because she was exhausted, and partly because she didn't want to be out here when it was dark and have a snake catch her unaware. Yet she was afraid because she didn't know how she and Preston were going to sleep cuddled up in that tent. As the day had worn on and she'd gotten to know Preston, she'd let herself relax and found he wasn't just irresistibly attractive; he was a funny and kind person.

They took turns using the bathroom, then waded into the pool to wash their faces and brush their teeth. Preston let her use the toothbrush first. It was gross that they had to share, but he wasn't a bad person to share with.

Once they'd dried off their faces, legs, and feet with the towel, Preston hung it over a bush and then unzipped the tent door. "Ladies first."

She forced a smile and took a deep breath. This was the moment she'd stressed about most of the day. She was exhausted, so hopefully she'd crash and not dwell on pressing against him in this small tent.

Ducking inside, she sat on the edge of the thin pad, covered with the soft fleece blanket, and waited for him to come in. Preston stepped inside, crouched over because it was so small. He zipped the flap closed.

"Zip that tight," she said. "No snakes in our tent."

He chuckled. "Finally safe from the snakes."

It was stuffy and warm in the tent, even though the window-type flap up high had been open. "Hopefully it'll cool off," she murmured.

"Hopefully." Preston sat down next to her. The tent was small, but it seemed to shrink even further. It was too dark to see more than his outline, so she couldn't read his expression as he turned toward her and murmured, "I don't want to make you uncomfortable, but we're going to have to get close."

"Too late on not making me uncomfortable."

He chuckled. "Oh, good. Let's figure out how to fit in here, then, so we can sleep."

"Okay," she squeaked out.

"Why don't you lie down; then I'll ... curl around you."

Oh my, that sounded much too intimate. Ally had no experience cuddling with a man. She couldn't even speak as she lay down on her side, trying to press her body back against the side of the tent so she'd take up as little space as possible. At least she was only five-four and she could stretch all the way out and not touch her head or feet to the tent wall.

Preston lay down and stretched out, but the tent was too short for him to completely stretch out, so his knees bent, pressing into her legs, and his chest brushed against her shoulder. Ally sucked in a breath. She realized right then she should've lain down facing away from him, but it was too late now as their bodies were inches apart and rolling away would be obvious.

The air in the tent seemed to crackle. She wished she was comfortable around men like her sisters, but she wasn't, and she could feel that her awkwardness was projecting onto him.

It was nice to lie down after such a long day, but the pad underneath them was thin and any slight movement would have them touching more places than their legs. She took shallow breaths, prayed for help from above to be able to sleep, and squeezed her eyes shut.

Long minutes passed with only her jagged breaths and his more even breathing filling the tent. His breath brushed her forehead time and again, and she longed to feel it intermingle with hers. The sound of birds and insects from outside were some accompaniment, but even the fears of the snake and the anguish of being stranded on this island were secondary to how uncomfortable she was in this tent. She didn't worry anymore that Preston might take advantage of the situation, but the seconds seemed unbearably long and awkward thanks to her own attraction to him and her worries that he couldn't possibly mean it when he complimented her or looked at her in that special way.

She had no clue how long they lay there motionless, but her breathing wasn't calming down. He had to know how uncomfortable she felt, how attracted she was to him, and how deep inside she only wanted him to pull her close. If only she could rest her head in the crook of his neck, feel his body against hers; then she wouldn't even care if she slept. Sheesh, her heart was thumping out of control at her silly fantasies. Her mom would be so disappointed in her unrealistic desires; she'd raised her girls to be independent and strong and never rely on anyone.

"Are you awake?" Preston murmured into the miniscule space between them.

Ally laughed uneasily. "What gave that away?"

Preston chuckled, and as he shifted closer, she felt his laughter against her own chest. "You're breathing ... a little fast. I'm sorry if I'm making you uncomfortable."

Why did he have to be such a nice guy? "It's not your fault," she said.

A few seconds passed before he said, "Tell me about your family."

"What? Why?"

Preston shifted his arm so it stretched above her head. Ally sucked in a breath. He wasn't even close to cuddling her, but she felt surrounded by him.

"I'd love to know more about you, Alyandra Heathrow." She could hear a smile in his voice, but it wasn't mocking; it was as if he was sincerely interested. They were in an alternate reality. No way Preston Steele would be interested in chubby Alyandra Heathrow in the real world. "I know about the driven, intelligent, and funny marketing manager. I'd like to know more about where you come from."

Ally cleared her throat, unsure how to share without *really* sharing. If he started to understand her family dynamic, he'd know why *I Feel Pretty* was so relatable to her. He'd acted surprised by that, saying something about how women were too hard on themselves and didn't appreciate how they could be beautiful in their own way. Could he truly believe that? Were his compliments not just empty? Could she be beautiful to him, in a different way than the rail-thin models he usually dated were?

"Well, I'm the oldest of three," she started. "My sisters, Shar and Kim, are ... adorable." That was putting it mildly. They were the most gorgeous, accomplished women she knew. She was very proud, and sometimes let herself be jealous.

"Like you," he murmured.

Ally's heart rate doubled and she was afraid she might hyperventilate. He needed to stop saying things like that, or she might believe they were true. "Um, yeah, we kind of look alike, the dark hair and coloring." She rushed on before he could say anything more. "My mom raised us to be strong women. She always said I had the brains, Shar had the cooking ability, and Kim had the talent with acting. Do you know Kim?"

"Yes. I remember her being in Disney shows, and I met her and her fiancé Colt Quinn through Gunner." He paused and then said, "I just realized that was the same party I met Sutton Smith at. Isn't it crazy that my brother is working for Sutton Smith?"

"Pretty crazy. That's who Colt works for too." The connection was interesting. She'd known Colt was a security specialist for the philanthropic billionaire Sutton Smith, but the realization that she was stranded on this island because of Gunner, who also worked for Sutton, felt surreal.

"So do you get along with your sisters?" Preston steered the topic back to her family.

"Not as teenagers." She smiled. "We fought over everything from wearing a certain shirt to who used up the last of the good hair gel. But we appreciate and love each other now." Her sisters would be mortified if they knew how petty she was, envious of them because their shapes were incredible and hers was ... too much. Kim had been so busy with her career and then lived in Costa Rica the past five years, so they didn't talk much, but Ally and Shar were very close. Shar was always telling Ally how beautiful she was and trying to convince Ally to give men a chance, saying silly things about men being interested in Ally. Ally appreciated her sister, but knew she only saw the good and couldn't possibly understand how insecure Ally was around men.

"And Kim's starring in that new chick flick coming out with Scarlett Lily," Preston said.

"Yeah, she's excited to get back into acting."

"Why'd she take such a long break?"

"Well, that's a crazy story. She had a stalker for over ten years, and she finally broke down, stopped acting, and moved to Costa Rica. Then Colt Quinn found her again—they'd dated before but he broke her heart—and he caught her stalker and she forgave him. Happily ever after and all of that. I'm condensing the story, a lot."

"You could tell me long drawn-out stories. We've got all night."

"I'm hoping to calm down in this miniscule, awkward space and actually get some shut-eye. I'm exhausted."

He chuckled. "I'm with you." Clearing his throat, he said, "Maybe if you ... laid your head on my shoulder, we could get more comfortable."

"Your arm would fall asleep with me lying on it."

"Aw, come on, don't insult my manliness."

"How is that insulting your manliness?" He had far too much manliness, and the rumble of his deep voice just reiterated that fact.

"A little thing like you, making my arm go to sleep? I'm tougher than that."

Instead of lying on his shoulder like he'd suggested, she pushed up to a seated position, wishing she could see his face clearly. "Do you mean any of the crap that spews out of that mouth of yours?"

"Excuse me?"

"I'm serious. Did your mother raise you to just schmooze

women, or are you really delusional enough to think I'm pretty and 'little'? Nobody in my life has called me little."

Preston's breath rushed out of him as if he'd been punched. "Are you kidding me?" He sat up abruptly, wrapped his arms around her, and pulled her into the circle of his embrace.

Now Ally's breath left her in a whoosh. She didn't return the hug, but she let him hold her close. Her heart was racing and she felt like she was going to explode, yet at the same time she felt calmer than she ever had. Preston's embrace truly was home to her, which was terrifying in and of itself. No way did they have a chance of dating once they went back to the real world.

"Look at how you fit in my arms. Can you feel it?" Preston asked, his breath heavy and warm against her forehead as he bent down close.

"It feels ... amazing," she admitted.

"It does," Preston agreed. "But don't you also notice how small you are in my arms?"

"That's only because you're huge," she flung back at him.

Preston shook his head. "I am bigger than most people, but you're not big at all. Your shape is incredible."

"Stop it." She tried to pull back, but his arms were firm around her. "Now I know you're just a lying jerk who only wants to get a little action because he's bored in this tropical prison."

"Whoa!" Preston released her. The tent was even more stifling and uncomfortable than it had been before. "Do you realize how many levels you've just insulted me on?"

"Do you realize I don't need to hear lies about my shape? I know I'm overweight, okay? I've worked my entire life to be fit, but I'm shaped different than my sisters. My aunt always called me 'big-boned.' It's fine. I can deal with the embarrassment, the rejection from men. It's fine, but please don't lie to me and claim my shape is 'incredible.' It's not fair or right to use your compliments to make me fall harder for you." If there weren't snakes outside, she'd run out of this tent right now. She wanted space so she could have a proper cry. Being in his arms was heaven, and she'd not only insulted him but revealed to him how low her confidence truly was.

"Ally." Preston sort of groaned out her name, and then he wrapped her up in his arms again. Ally didn't even try to resist. "Oh, Ally. Who, besides your aunt, misguided you and made you think you were overweight? I love your shape. You have perfect curves, and you're soft and feminine. What kind of a monster would put it in your head that you're not attractive?"

Ally heard his words, but processing them was an entirely different beast. He not only didn't think she was fat; he thought she was perfect, soft, and feminine? What kind of delusional reality was she living in right now? Maybe it was all a dream and she'd wake up soon. She wouldn't miss the snakes or being stranded, but being in Preston's arms was a dream she didn't ever want to wake up from.

"Ally," he started again. "You have to understand something. I would never lie to you. Do you believe me?"

She rested her head in the crook of his neck and let her arms make their way around his back.

Preston was the one breathing faster now. He tenderly kissed her forehead and said, "Please say you believe me. I don't like living in a world where you think you're not beautiful and you also think I'm some lying man trying to take advantage of you."

"It's a world with snakes too, so it's really horrible," she tried to joke.

Preston laughed, and that made her feel better. She needed to take a leap of faith here, to trust him. Yet she'd seen all those pictures of him with thin, gorgeous models. How could he be attracted to her as well? Didn't men have a certain type they found attractive? She'd gotten used to a world where that type was never her.

"Please trust me," Preston whispered.

Ally swallowed. They might be stuck on this island until they both were killed by a snake. Preston's voice was sincere, and his reputation for honesty was impeccable. Every part of her screamed that if she couldn't trust this man, she might never trust any man.

"I will," she said. "I will trust you." She repeated it more forcefully.

"Thank you," Preston breathed. "I would never take advantage of you, Ally, but you are the most incredibly beautiful woman I've ever met, and if you can't feel how attracted I am to you, I must be doing something wrong." He cradled her in tighter against him.

Ally ran her hands over the muscles in his back. "You're doing everything right," she admitted. Now if only he'd kiss her, but somehow she sensed he was too honorable to try, especially since she'd demanded earlier today that he not touch her. She'd claimed he was lying about how attractive she was so that he could take advantage of her. Kissing her right now wouldn't work, and she knew it, though she still wanted to kiss him very, very badly.

"I think it would be smart if we lay down and slept. Tomorrow, when we're not cuddled in a too-small tent, I'll tell you more about how attractive you are, but right now my self-control is at its limits."

Ally's heart walloped against her chest again. He was the undeniably attractive one and she'd give anything to kiss the night away, but she loved first of all that she was testing his self-control, and second of all that he was strong enough to control himself. Preston was incredible, and she suddenly felt that being stranded with him was a gift from above.

Preston slid down on his back and cuddled her against his side. Her head fit perfectly against the defined muscles of his shoulder.

"You're sure your arm won't fall asleep?" she asked.

"Don't insult my manliness," he reminded her, chuckling.

Ally laughed too. Her right arm was trapped between their bodies and might well lose blood flow during the night, but her left arm was free. She cautiously placed it on his chest. He started breathing quicker, and she could feel his heart thumping under her palm. The smooth skin and musculature of his chest were perfect. "Is that okay?" she whispered.

"Better than okay." His voice was tight and controlled, but he tenderly kissed her forehead again. "Good night, Ally."

Ally closed her eyes and savored the feel of him against her, waiting for his heartbeat to calm under her palm. She drifted off to sleep with a smile on her face, loving that his pulse raced because of her.

# CHAPTER TEN

Preston woke to birds twittering outside and the most incredible sensation—Ally snuggled against his chest. His left arm was indeed asleep, but he would never tell her that. The sun was up and the tent was getting hot again. It had cooled off late in the night, and as Ally's breathing had relaxed, he'd forced himself to not focus on her soft shape in his arms and her hand on his chest. Eventually it'd worked and he'd drifted off.

Last night had opened his eyes to a reality he was still struggling to comprehend: Ally thought she was overweight. He recognized that most of the women he'd dated were much too thin and society was crazy about being perfectly skinny or fit, but that didn't make Ally unattractive. She had the most irresistible curves and a gorgeous face. To him, she wasn't even close to overweight. He wondered if it was society and the media that skewed women's images of themselves like this, or if someone in her life had said or done something to make her feel like less.

Someone besides her crazy aunt. Big-boned. What a joke. He wanted to get to the bottom of it. He smiled grimly as he realized they had time ... lots and lots of time.

Ally's eyelashes fluttered as her eyes opened. Her beautiful face curved in a smile as she saw him staring at her. "Good morning," she murmured.

"It really is," he said. That was crazy, as they were stuck in this insane situation, but he thought this was a great morning as well.

"Don't sound so shocked." Her smile grew. "Is your arm asleep?"

"Nope," he lied, trying to discreetly clench and unclench his fist to get some blood flow back to his arm.

"Well, lucky you. Mine's a throbbing mess." She shifted away from him, sat up, and moved her right arm, which had been trapped between their bodies.

He sat up too and stretched. He immediately missed her cuddled in his arms, but they might have an opportunity this sunny day to do more than simply hold each other. He wanted to kiss her, now that it wasn't nighttime and he wasn't so overwhelmed with her tempting form pressed close. It would be much easier to stay in control if they were standing up and out in the sunshine. He wanted to brush his teeth, convince her how amazing she was to him, then ask if he could kiss her. He would show her exactly how attractive she was to him, and not just because of her looks—her great attitude, funny personality, and success all drew him in as well.

"I've got to pee like a racehorse," Ally shot out.

Preston chuckled. "Well, don't let me stop you from doing that."

She crouched next to the tent zipper, undid it, and screamed. Preston leapt to his feet, pushing her behind him. A snake sat coiled just outside the tent, staring at him.

Preston zipped the tent up quickly, then pulled her against him and scooted them to the other side of the tent. Unfortunately, the tent wasn't big enough, or thick enough, to give the illusion of much safety. Ally buried her head against his chest, and he was distracted temporarily by her warm breath against his bare flesh.

"I hate snakes, I hate snakes," she muttered over and over again.

"It's okay. It'll go away," Preston tried to reassure her. He wasn't fond of snakes either, and that snake was between him and the knife he'd cleaned in the pool, after killing that snake's friend or brother.

Squeezing his eyes shut, he prayed audibly, "Please protect us, Lord. Please let the snake go on its way. Amen."

"Amen," Ally repeated. She clung to his lower back and Preston held her close against him, both of their legs tucked up underneath their bodies to try to stay as far away from that snake as possible. Long moments passed, and Preston waited for the snake to snap at the tent and rip clean through it. Nothing happened. Preston thought he heard the snake slither away, but he couldn't be sure. He'd stand up and check through the higher window, in a minute. Right now he was going to hold Ally and help her calm down.

"Do you want to hit me again to make yourself feel better?" he tried to joke.

She looked up at him, her dark eyes so vulnerable and beautiful. "I kind of did like hitting you." Pulling back slightly, she looked over his chest, then frowned. "You don't even have a bruise."

He chuckled. "I told you, little thing like you couldn't hurt me."

"Don't call me little," she threw back at him, but she was smiling.

"Pint-sized, teeny-tiny, absolutely beautiful, and hilarious, small woman."

She leaned back and softly punched him in the stomach, grinning broadly. "Stop it."

"You call me names now," he said, happy to be distracted from that snake. He prayed that it was gone.

"Egotistical, overly muscled, absolutely beautiful, and kind, massive man."

"You obviously didn't have brothers. Your insults are lame." Preston chuckled. What he wouldn't give to kiss her right now. But first they needed to get out of this tent and brush their teeth.

"Nope, but sisters can be vicious, so don't push me."

Preston's smile slid away. Would the famous Kim Heathrow or Ally's other sister have demeaned her because she wasn't as thin as them? That made no sense to him. His brothers teased and wrestled and made fun of each other, but it was understood that they loved each other deeply and they would always have each other's backs. True, Preston was a world-class athlete, so confidence hadn't been hard to come by; from the time he was small, he was showered with praise from his parents and coaches. But he'd never compared himself to his brothers, only cheered for them.

"I am going to pee my pants," Ally declared.

Preston couldn't resist kissing her forehead. He'd done that a lot and liked it a lot, but it was past time to kiss her lips. "You're adorable, you know that?"

"Adorable?" Ally fluttered her eyelashes at him. "I'm glad you think so. When I pee on you, will you still think that?"

Preston shrugged. "Brothers, remember? I've been peed on before."

"Gross!"

Preston couldn't stop laughing. Who cared about a snake and being stranded? He had Ally to make him laugh and to tease with, and soon he was going to show her exactly how attracted he was to her when he kissed her.

He released her and stretched to look out the window. No snake anywhere in view. "It's gone," he said.

"Are you sure?"

"I'll go first to make sure."

Ally stood and gave him a fierce hug, kind of awkward with them bent over, but he loved that she'd initiated the contact. "You're my hero. Please don't get bitten by a snake. I have no clue how to suck venom out of a wound."

"Oh, it's easy. Just get the knife, make some cuts, suck, and spit. Oh, and don't forget to tourniquet above it."

"So gross! You cut that snake's brother apart with that knife; you'd get poisoned and be dead for sure. Don't get bitten!" She released him and pushed him slightly. "Now let's go so I don't pee in our sleeping spot."

Preston smiled and slowly unzipped the tent. The snake was indeed gone, and he said a prayer of gratitude and another prayer that a snake wouldn't catch them unaware again and they could be safe today. He stood outside the tent and stretched, searching for a snake, or something worse. He wondered if Carlos had known this island was overrun with snakes. Carlos probably did know—he'd found an island with a great source of fresh water, so he must've explored it.

"All clear?" Ally squeaked out.

"Yes."

She eased out of the tent, dancing slightly. "Okay, you turn your head, because I am not going far."

He laughed and turned to face the tent. "Be careful."

"You got it."

He liked her, a lot. At this moment, he wouldn't complain if they were stuck here for a good, long time, even with the snakes.

# CHAPTER ELEVEN

Ally enjoyed the day with Preston as much as any day she could remember. There were no more too-close snake sightings, and they very carefully explored their small island. They found mango and guava trees that bore ripe and delicious fruit. They tried, and failed, to start a fire by spinning sticks. They walked the perimeter of the island again, staying close to the sand but still in the shade to get some exercise, talking about his career and schooling and hers, family and friends, and the Patriots. He was impressed that she was such a football geek.

They went for a swim in the ocean, swimming back and forth in front of the spot where the creek went up to their camp. Ally loved how the salty water made her feel buoyant, but it was awkward to swim in the big T-shirt. She wasn't taking it off, though. When they went back up to their camp spot, Preston said, "Do you want to shower in the waterfall first?"

"We can do it together," she said. His eyes widened, and she realized what she'd suggested. "It's not like either of us are taking off more clothes."

His gaze was practically smoldering now, but all he said was, "You're going to shower in the T-shirt?"

She nodded. "I need to wash it anyway. It'll dry before we go to sleep." The thought of being in that tent again, all cuddled in his arms, made her hotter than the sun. She'd loved him holding her last night, and she loved feeling so close to him. This incredible and irresistible man thought she was attractive. She wanted to jump and sing.

"Okay." He grabbed the little bag of toiletries, and they waded into the pool together. Ally felt all lit up as they stood close by each other and took turns rinsing their hair under the small waterfall. The setting was incredible with the lush greenery and water trickling down and the handsome, shirtless man next to her. My, oh my, he was beautiful. The most amazing part was that he thought she was beautiful. Her mom wouldn't like that it mattered to her—she'd always taught them to focus on their talents and their brains—but Ally knew Preston liked her personality as well. He seemed to like all of her.

Preston opened the bottle of shampoo and squeezed some into her hand. She started lathering it into her hair, smiling at him as he stared at her. His stare was longing, fiery, inspiring.

"May I?" he asked in a deep voice that pulsed through her.

Ally slowly lowered her hands and said, "Wash my hair?"

"Yes."

She couldn't speak, overwhelmed by attraction. She nodded and he stepped in closer. Raising his arms, he started massaging her scalp. Ally was in awe of how beautiful the musculature of his upper body was, but she was quickly distracted by the insanely good feeling of him massaging her hair and scalp. Tingles of pleasure radiated from her head down. She might have moaned softly, but she hoped she'd held it in.

Closing her eyes, she gave in to the incredible feeling of his large palms working their way through her hair and gently untangling it. Who knew how long passed as he went over her head time and again with his fingers and palms. He tilted her head back under the water, and she reveled in the shampoo washing out as his hands kept working their magic.

Some water trailed over her face and along her cheek. She blinked her eyes open. Preston's gaze was heavy on her, so warm and tempting she knew she couldn't resist him any longer. Why would she want to resist him?

She wrapped her arms around his lower back and tilted her head up. His hands were still in her hair as he pulled her slightly away from the stream of water and up and into his body. His eyes swept over her, full of tenderness and desire. Ally's entire body was on fire. She'd never had a man look at her like that, especially not a man like Preston. He was good, kind, funny, smart, talented, and incredibly handsome.

"Ally?" he whispered. "May I kiss you?"

Ally's stomach hopped with happiness. He not only wanted to kiss her; he remembered that she'd made him agree not to kiss her, until he asked. "Yes, please," she whispered back.

He gave her his irresistible grin; then his head bowed to hers and he didn't waste any time as he claimed her lips with his. Ally's body seemed to soar off the ground as his hands worked their way down her back to encircle her waist and her lips were lit up from the sheer pleasure of his mouth on hers. He took his time kissing her, savoring every part of her lips and keeping her body tightly clasped against his.

When he finally pulled back, Ally realized that it wasn't just his kiss that gave her the soaring sensation; she was indeed suspended in the air as he held her tightly against him. He gently lowered her to her feet and pressed his forehead against hers. "I've been wanting to do that all day," he said quietly.

"Well, why have you been wasting time waiting?" she asked breathily.

He chuckled. "I wanted to make sure that you wanted me as much as I want you."

Ally's jaw dropped and her eyes widened. "I've got you so beat on the wanting thing."

Preston shook his head. "Not even close." Then he was kissing her again, and not even a snake could've pulled them apart.

---

The rest of the afternoon and evening just got better and better. They talked and kissed and simply savored being together. When night fell, they were safely in the tent, wrapped in each other's arms. Ally barely remembered the reality of their situation and the fact that a snake might get one of them at any time.

"Ally?" Preston whispered roughly.

"Hmm," she said.

"Two things. No, three."

"Okay." She smiled. "One?"

"I'm sorry I was so rude about your marketing idea that night in Bucky's garden."

Ally hadn't even thought about work or the real world today. "It's okay. I'm probably too focused on the marketability of everything. It's impressive what you and your family do, not wanting any glory for giving. I love that about you."

"Thank you, but your idea is great too. I got on my philosophical high horse, and it's silly. Any idea that can help make someone's dreams come true, and bring more awareness to stories that touch people's hearts, is amazing. If it helps sell out the stadium, I will be grateful for that too. More fans cheering for me, right?"

Ally laughed. "Thank you, Preston. If we ever get back, maybe we'll run with it."

He nodded. "Good plan."

A few beats passed and she said, "Two?"

He didn't say anything for a few seconds then asked quietly, "Who made you feel like less?"

"Like less?"

"Like you aren't the complete package? You're smart, talented, funny, and beautiful, but someone in your life, besides your crazy aunt, made you feel ... bigger?"

Ally's stomach plummeted. She didn't want to get into this discussion, but she found she trusted Preston more than she'd ever trusted anyone, her sisters included. "There was a kid in middle school who I liked. He kissed me, then he told everybody how gross it was because I was fat."

"What an idiot. He was probably just being a stupid teenager."

She hummed in acknowledgment, not telling him about the other two boys who'd basically done the same thing to her and how she'd stayed far away from boys after that. She continued, "My mom was focused on each of us being successful women, and that was supposed to have nothing to do with our exterior. I heard her a few times telling my sister Kim how beautiful she was and that it would help her career. She and my dad never once told me I was attractive, but I did overhear her telling my dad how sad it was that I was ... chubby, when my sisters had such gorgeous shapes."

He grunted in disgust. "That's not true at all. You realize that, right?"

"You realize you're the only one who thinks that?" She leaned in close and tenderly kissed his neck.

He let out a moan and his grip on her tightened. "Don't do that, or I can't have a rational conversation."

"Maybe I don't want a rational conversation."

Preston laughed but stopped abruptly when she kissed his neck again, then slowly trailed kisses along his jawline and up to his mouth. She softly pressed her lips to his. Preston returned the kiss—oh, how he returned it. His kiss told her more than even his words that he was attracted to her, that her teenage rejections and her mom's philosophies didn't matter. What they had together was real, and he cared for her and wanted her. She was safe with him.

"Ally." He broke away and leaned back. "We need to stop. I have to tell you about number three ..."

"Why would we stop?" She kissed him again. Number three could wait. She wanted to kiss him all night; what could possibly be wrong with that? They were both rational and in-control adults. They wouldn't go farther than kissing.

Preston's mouth hungrily moved against her own, and she lost all track of time and accountability. She only wanted to keep kissing him and experiencing these incredible sensations. Then he did something that shocked her but also set her body on fire: he rolled her onto her back and pressed his body on top of hers. The kiss continued, taking on a life of its own, and her body responded to the pressure of his. She'd never known desire for a man existed like this.

Preston yanked away from her and said, "No! I can't." He pulled away from her and rolled completely over, turning his back to her.

Ally's stomach was still full of heat and her breath was coming in fast gulps. What had just happened? She lay there for a few seconds, trying to register how he could've kissed her so hungrily and then torn away from her like that.

She leaned up and put a hand on his upper back. He sucked in a loud breath. "Preston?" she questioned timidly. "What's wrong?"

"Please, Ally. You don't understand ... men."

What in the world did that mean? "No, I don't," she agreed, but she thought she understood him. What had yanked him away from her?

"You're so innocent." He pushed out a breath. "I'll explain ... tomorrow. Please don't touch me right now," he said in a controlled voice that terrified her. He was pulling away from her emotionally as well as physically, and it hurt.

Ally pulled her hand back. She rolled the opposite way and faced the tent wall. What had happened? She'd been consumed with his kiss one second, and then he'd turned from her and didn't even want her to touch him? Her world was spinning. She knew Preston was a good man, an honorable man, and she'd kept making him kiss her when he wanted to stop. He'd probably realized it wasn't fair to lead her on when he'd never want to be with her outside this island. A voice in her head reminded her of the painful reality of her teenage and college years. Men like Preston didn't want a woman like her. Her softer, bigger shape had disgusted Preston or maybe him saying she was innocent was only code for her not knowing how to kiss correctly. He'd let himself kiss and hold her, and now he was regretting it and was shutting her out.

Squeezing her eyes shut tight, she couldn't keep the tears from sliding out of the corners of her eyelids. She cried silently, hugging herself and praying desperately that they'd be rescued tomorrow. She couldn't stand to see the rejection in Preston's eyes in the light of day.

# CHAPTER TWELVE

Preston spent an absolutely miserable night curled away from Ally, cringing every time her soft, irresistible body brushed his from behind. He'd almost lost control, and with the most amazing woman he'd ever met. His parents had drilled it into him that if you loved someone, you loved them more than your selfish desires and waited for marriage to be intimate, and you never, ever took advantage of a woman. He didn't know if what he felt for Ally was love, but it was definitely stronger than anything he'd ever felt for a woman. He wanted to protect her, laugh with her, explore and make memories with her, and touch and kiss her. Only her. He thought she might be the woman for him, and he'd almost pushed her too far physically last night. It was even worse because Ally was both innocent and vulnerable, obviously inexperienced with dating and ignorant of how attractive she was to him. As soon as she woke up, he'd explain to her how irresistible and impressive she was, and that he'd turned away last night to stay in control.

Even with the sun shining bright and a new day upon them, he was still worried he would lose control again. How long could he sleep in this tent with her and never take it further? Not long at all if they kissed like they had last night.

They needed to make some rules. That was it. This morning. He'd get out of this tent fast, and then, over breakfast, he'd explain how tempting she was to him and how they could only kiss in the daylight, standing up. That would be good. And he'd pray hard that he wouldn't be such a weak fool ever again. He'd pray even harder that they'd get rescued soon so he could date her properly, see where these incredible feelings for her could go. She was the complete package to him and he wanted more time to get to know her funny personality and watch her succeed at her career and simply be there for her.

He sat up and glanced at Ally. Her back was still to him and she was curled against the other side of the tent. Could she still be asleep? He didn't want to wake her if she was getting some much-needed rest, but she looked amazing in that too-big T-shirt, her dark hair spilling around her and onto the smooth skin of her neck. Maybe he could just lean around and kiss her cheek and still keep things chaste. Brush the hair away and sample the curve of her neck.

No! He couldn't even keep his own self-imposed rules. No kissing in this tent, ever again. Crouching, he looked out the window of the tent, prepared to see that snake again, but what he saw wasn't a dangerous reptile. What he saw sneering at him was much, much worse.

One of the men from Carlos's yacht—the one who spoke English, if he remembered correctly—was glowering at him with a pistol pointed at the mesh window. "Come out nice and slow, mi amigo," the man said.

Preston nodded, hoping he could keep Ally out of this. But she stirred quickly next to him, and he realized she hadn't been asleep at all. Her eyes were wild as she jumped to her feet and took in the man and then turned to Preston, fear evident in the beautiful lines of her face.

"Preston?" she whispered.

"It's okay," he said.

"Hello, mujer hermosa," the man murmured. "Happy to see you. Unzip the tent," he growled at Preston.

Preston didn't know what else to do but obey. Maybe he could jump the guy and knock the gun from his hand. He unzipped the tent, then slowly eased outside. Reaching for Ally, he held on to her arm and helped her out of the tent, keeping her behind him.

"Don't hide, mi bella," the man crooned.

"What are you doing here?" Preston asked, his eyes flitting to the gun aimed at his chest.

"Your brother come."

Preston's stomach hopped. Gunner had come for them? Thank heavens. Preston would dismantle this guy, then go find his brother. "Is he close?" he asked.

"He kill Carlos, big fight on the yacht last night. I escape in little boat. Nobody come. I know this island. I come to take the woman and kill you."

Preston's palms dampened. He could throttle this guy if he could get around the gun. "Well, that sounds simple, and nasty," Preston said. Had this guy escaped pursuit? Was there any hope Gunner would come for them? After he took this guy out, Preston would have to figure out which direction to travel in whatever boat the man had come on, or maybe get the stupid branches to do more than smoke when he twisted them.

Ally eased around to Preston's side. He pulled her back.

"Let me go," she whispered.

"No."

She rose up on tiptoes and whispered into his ear. "Tackle him when I distract him."

Preston's body trembled. It was a simple plan, but so many things could go wrong. He didn't have much to lose, as the guy had already said he was going to kill him; the bullet could hit his chest any moment. But what if Ally got hit in the crossfire? Yet would Ally want to live with what this man would do to her? Preston had to protect her, and her distraction would up his chances of succeeding in taking the guy out. He squeezed her arm, then released it.

Ally stepped around Preston and made the most seductive look he'd ever seen in a woman's eyes, and it was even more appealing because it was Ally. Yet it wasn't directed at him, but at the man pointing a gun at him. His stomach boiled with jealousy, even though he knew she wasn't really after this guy.

"I'm so glad you came," Ally said, all sweet and irresistible. "I've been thinking of you and wanting to get away from him." She pointed at Preston and took a large step away from him and toward the man. Touching his face, she murmured, "I've been waiting for you."

The man hung loosely to the gun as his eyes focused on Ally. Preston hated that she was touching him, and then the man used his free hand to trail his fingers down Ally's arm. "Muy bella," he said.

Ally was Preston's girl, and no one had the right to touch her but him. The fierce protectiveness he felt toward her swelled until it was almost overwhelming. He blinked, knowing he had to keep a clear head and not let the jealousy overtake him.

The man's eyes were fixed on her as she kept talking about how she'd noticed him on the boat, how handsome he was, etc. Preston waited until the man's grip on the gun loosened and it was no longer aimed at him. He leapt, putting his 4.3 40-yard combine skills to the test. He rammed the man from the side, knocking him into the ground and away from Ally. The pistol went off, and he was terrified that a stray bullet might have gotten Ally.

He grabbed the man's hand and slammed it into the ground as he jammed his own forehead into the side of the man's head. The man howled in pain and released the gun.

Preston was seeing stars from hitting the man so hard with his head. How had that not knocked the guy out?

Ally's hand darted in and she grabbed the gun.

"No, Ally!" Preston didn't want her anywhere near this man or the gun.

The man bucked his body and slammed his free hand into Preston's temple; there was something solid in his grip that had Preston swaying and hardly able to keep his head. The darkness was encroaching on Preston, but he wasn't going to pass out and fail Ally. He rolled his body weight on top of the guy and punched him in the side of the head. The man's hand came up to hit him again just as Preston saw the rock in his palm. He hit Preston in the temple with it. Stars exploded and the world started going black. Preston slid to the side, nausea threatening as he tried to hold on to consciousness. The rock was coming at him again. This hit might finish him off.

"Stop!" Ally yelled. "Or I'll shoot."

The man's fist stopped in midair, and he looked at Ally in surprise. "You won't shoot," he said snidely.

"Move, Preston," Ally commanded.

Preston slid off of the man and onto his knees. How could he protect Ally when he couldn't even see straight?

The man sprang up and was raising the rock to smash it into Preston's head again. The gun went off, and the man screeched in pain and sprang away from Preston.

Preston stared through bleary eyes at the man and Ally. She stood, shaking slightly, with the gun still aimed at the man. "I told you I'd shoot."

She was so incredibly brave. Preston couldn't believe she'd actually shot the guy.

Blood spurted from the guy's shoulder. "Loco señorita," he cursed.

"I'll do it again," Ally warned. She came close to Preston and knelt down next to him, still clinging to the gun. "Are you okay?"

"Dizzy," he admitted. He was going to pass out or puke. They needed to ... tie the guy up and go to the beach and make a signal fire or something. Gunner was close by, but Preston could hardly keep his nausea down or his head clear. He'd had concussions before, but nothing had felt this debilitating.

"You're incredible, Ally," Preston whispered. His ears rang from a roar and another shot, and his head exploded as the rock caught him in the temple again. Then everything went dark.

# CHAPTER THIRTEEN

Ally was panicking hard-core. Preston was passed out, and she had no clue how much damage the guy had done to his head. She'd shot the man again, this time hitting his leg. The man was glaring at her from not far enough away, as she'd yelled at him to get back or she'd finish him off this time. Yet she had no clue how to keep him under control, even with a bullet wound to his shoulder and leg. She had no rope to tie him up with. With her luck, another snake would appear. Maybe the creature would go after the wounded man. Did snakes sense blood? No, that was sharks, right?

Last night had been horrible as she'd felt confused and basically rejected by Preston, but today was even worse. He had said she was incredible before he passed out, but his safety was the bigger concern right now. She felt for a pulse, and luckily, he still had one. He'd taken more than enough hits to the head as a football player. How long would he be passed out? How did she treat a head injury? What if he didn't wake up? Her heart constricted at the thought. She needed Preston, in so many ways.

The man groaned in pain and she clung to the gun, pointing it at him. Thank heavens the gun had been loaded with no safety on and all she'd had to do was aim and fire. She shook slightly, realizing she could've killed the guy instead of hitting his shoulder, but thankfully she hadn't. No matter how vile he was, she didn't want that on her conscience.

"You." She pointed the gun at the man. "Go get in that tent." She gestured toward it with her head.

He nodded, stood with a grimace, and shuffled toward the tent. The look in his eyes was murderous, but he appeared compliant. He reached the tent, and she suddenly realized she was telling a bleeding man to get her safe spot all dirty. She needed to get Preston in there and nurse him back to health, without the worry of a snake slithering over him.

"Wait," she said. "Go sit under the waterfall. The water will wash the blood away." It sounded like an okay theory, and with him in the water, it would be harder for him to rush her while she checked on Preston.

"Loca," he muttered again, but he walked toward the waterfall.

As he approached, he wasn't looking at her, but he was getting too close. She started to back away. He ducked low and dove at her legs, knocking her off her feet and against the hard ground. The breath whooshed out of her, and pain radiated through her back. Ally clung to the gun and smacked him in the head with it. He shouted in pain and reached for the gun.

A snake slithered from the undergrowth and struck the man's shoulder with his teeth. The man cried out and Ally screamed. He grabbed the snake and hurled it into the jungle. Ally hit him in the temple as hard as she could with the grip of the gun. He sank down to the ground. Ally scrambled to her feet. He wasn't out cold, but he was definitely stunned. She scurried away from him and toward Preston. "Please be okay. Please wake up."

Preston didn't stir. He was completely out. She rested a hand on his shoulder, drawing comfort from his warm flesh, and kept an eye on their attacker. Her gaze kept darting around for that snake. How could she keep the man under control and somehow doctor Preston? Would she have to kill the man to keep him from attacking them again?

Crashing noises from the bush startled her. She gasped and stood in front of Preston, aiming the gun at the new threat. Had more of Carlos's men found them? "Stop or I'll shoot!" she yelled in what she hoped was a threatening voice.

The footsteps stopped, but a man yelled, "Preston? Alyandra?" He sounded American.

"Who are you?" she demanded, her body trembling as she clung to the gun, wishing Preston would wake up.

"Gunner Steele," the man said.

"Oh, thank heavens." Ally sank to the ground next to Preston. She cradled his head against her chest, and his eyelids fluttered open. "We're saved," she told him. "Are you okay?"

"Can we proceed?" Gunner called.

"Yes!" Ally yelled back.

Preston blinked up at her. "You're so incredible," he slurred.

She couldn't resist kissing him quickly, but pulled back when he didn't really return it and she heard chuckles. The men filtering into the clearing looked like a tough bunch of military dudes. Two men led them: a guy who resembled Preston, and a tall, regal-looking man who looked like James Bond.

"Secure him," James Bond said.

Preston's brother hurried to him and Ally, staring seriously at both of them. "What happened to him?" he asked.

"He got hit in the head with a rock ... a few times." Ally suddenly felt embarrassment swoop in. Preston had rejected her last night, and here she was acting like they were a couple because they'd gone through something terrifying. She was thrilled to be rescued and that he'd awoken, but it meant real life was back, and part of real life was the reality that she and Preston weren't a match. Not in the hard, cold world she lived in, and not with the way he'd turned his back on her last night.

Preston gave her a loopy smile. He looked groggy and not like himself. "I'm good." He was still slurring his words. "I'm used to hits in the head. I'm a football player."

Gunner arched his eyebrows. "Yeah, you sound good, bro. Let's get you two out of here. We've got to get him to a medic."

Another man offered his arm to Ally. She took it and happily handed over the gun. Gunner, along with a guy burlier than any football player, helped Preston to his feet. Preston leaned heavily on his brother.

"Blimey, looks like the two of you got yourselves into a dodgy mess." James Bond came over and extended his hand to Ally. "Sutton Smith."

She shook his hand. "Nice to meet you. Ally Heathrow."

"I know who you are. Kim's sister." He gave her a kind smile. "Are you ready to go home?"

"Yes, sir," she said, but inside she was churning. Home. A home without Preston. Glancing over at him, she cringed when his head lolled to the side. She hoped he was okay. She knew their futures wouldn't coincide—no more than professionally, anyway. She'd known it even when he'd been holding her and kissing her last night, but she pushed that pain and longing away and concentrated on praying that he'd be okay.

# CHAPTER FOURTEEN

Preston awoke in an uncomfortable bed with too-white walls, wrinkling his nose at the stench of antiseptic. Blinking to clear his vision, he saw his brother Jex asleep in a chair. He looked more uncomfortable than Preston felt.

"Jex," he squeaked out of his dry throat.

Jex sat up quickly and then held his head. "Oh. I feel almost as bad as you look."

Preston laughed, but that hurt his throat worse. "Water?"

"Ice chips." Jex stood and rattled the cup. He spoon-fed Preston a bite.

Preston sucked on them as he pushed the button to raise his bed to a seated position. He reached for the cup. "I'm not an invalid. What am I doing in a hospital?"

Jex handed over the cup and rubbed at his beard. "Well, bro. You were stranded on an island with a beautiful woman."

"Thanks. I remember that part." At least some of it. A lot of the memories were fuzzy, especially how they'd gotten rescued. "Where is she?"

Jex shrugged. "I'd assume with her family. Her sister gets married tomorrow. They canceled the wedding, but then when you two got rescued, I guess they put it back on."

"Oh." That made sense. Her family needed her, but he felt like he needed her more. It was selfish, but he wanted Ally by his side.

His memories of the island were bleary, but he remembered their first, incredible kiss by the waterfall, and he remembered how hard he'd fallen for her. There was also something tickling at the back of his mind, something that felt uncomfortable and awkward. Had she fallen for him too, or had she rejected him and he'd blocked it out because it was too painful? Was that the real reason she wasn't here?

"What's wrong with me?" he asked.

"Doc says bad concussion. You might have temporary amnesia. You'll be okay. You were a little slow before, so this is nothing new."

"Thanks, bro. How soon can I get out of here?"

Jex shrugged. "I think tomorrow."

"I need to get out now." He had to get to Ally. He wished he could remember everything that transpired between them. He wished he had her phone number.

"Patience, my boy, patience." Jex gave him his easy grin.

Normally Preston would laugh at Jex's lame line, but right now he had no patience. "I need to talk to Ally. Can you get me my phone and her phone number?" Her sister needed her for her wedding day; that was the only reason they were apart. No matter how much he wanted her by his side, he wanted her to be happy most of all. He had to at least make sure she knew how impressive she was to him. Some things were spotty in his memory, but he could remember clearly that she hadn't felt good about herself, and he wanted to reassure her from now until the end of time that she was perfect to him.

"Um, your phone's probably been destroyed by that Carlos dude. I'll work on getting you a new phone and finding her number. Can you relax so I don't get in trouble with the nurses? Some of them are pretty cute."

Preston rolled his eyes. Only Jex would find a date in a hospital.

The door swung open and the sweetest voice cried, "My Preston!" Lottie rushed in and made it to the side of his bed. "Nurses say you look awake."

Preston opened his arms. "Hi, princess."

Lottie snuggled in as best she could with the bar hitting her in the stomach. "You okay, my bro?"

"I'm good, Lottie. Glad to see you, that's for sure." He kissed her forehead, and a memory of holding Ally and kissing her forehead surfaced. He'd loved having her in his arms, her soft flesh under his lips.

The rest of the family filtered in, interrupting his daydreams of Ally. His parents, Gunner, Slade, and Mae crowded into the hospital room. Slade's fiancé had a funny shirt on that read, *I'd give up chocolate but I'm no quitter.*

Preston laughed at the shirt as she gave him a one-arm hug. "Did you bring me any chocolate?"

"No, but I smuggled in a Diet Coke with passionfruit syrup and fresh lime. Want a sip?" She held the drink up and Preston took a long sip. The sweet and tart cola taste felt like heaven in his mouth. No, that wasn't true. It wasn't even close to as heavenly as Ally.

"You're a saint," he told Mae.

Mae winked. "He tells me that all the time."

Slade chuckled. "Yes, I do."

His mom moved in for a second hug. She clung to him, tears messing up her usually perfect makeup. "I still can't believe you were kidnapped and stranded on an island." She shot a dark glare at Gunner. "And I can't believe one of my sons wouldn't tell me the truth about what he was doing."

Gunner didn't appear fazed. He was the most serious of the bunch, and nothing really riled him. "It was so I could do deeper undercover jobs and not be recognized, and to keep all of you safe."

"Oh, that obviously didn't work," his mom shot at him.

"Mama, be nice," Lottie admonished. She went to Gunner and wrapped her arms around his waist. "I love my boys."

Gunner hugged her back, finally smiling. "We all love you, Lottie." He met Preston's gaze over her head. "I'm sorry."

Preston shook his head, a lingering headache making the movement hurt. "It was Carlos's fault, not yours. You got him, then?"

"Yes, and his brother, the guy he kidnapped you for, is awaiting trial for human trafficking and murder."

"That's good."

The conversation drifted to Preston's recovery, then came around to Slade and Mae's upcoming wedding. While Mae and his mom discussed flowers, with lots of input from Lottie, Preston said, "Gunner?"

His brother quickly strode to his bedside. "Yeah?"

"Can you get me a phone and get me Ally's number?"

"What? You don't trust me?" Jex asked.

"Gunner has better connections." Preston winked. "Also, are you going to Kim Heathrow and Colt Quinn's wedding tomorrow?"

"I have an invite." Gunner shrugged. He was the most serious of Preston's brothers, and the most antisocial. He hated events.

"Can I be your 'plus-one'?"

Gunner finally cracked half of a grin. "You can't pull off the high heels."

Preston smiled and finally relaxed into the bed. "Yeah, right, like you could say no to anything I ask right now."

Gunner acknowledged that with a lift of his eyebrows and incline of his head. He would get him the phone and Ally's number, and if Preston couldn't convince her to come see him before tomorrow, he was walking into that wedding and finding her. He didn't care what the doctors said.

# CHAPTER FIFTEEN

Ally was swept into wedding preparations so quickly that she almost felt like her time on the island with Preston hadn't even happened. Her family had grilled her with questions and overwhelmed her with hugs when she was escorted home by Sutton Smith's men. It had been hard to watch Preston be whisked away in a medivac without her, but it wasn't her place to insist she stay with him.

Kim and Colt had postponed the wedding when she'd gone missing, but luckily Sutton had kept their disappearance pretty quiet and Ally had been able to insist that they proceed with the wedding. She was fine, except for her broken heart, and no one but Preston would ever know about that. So she focused on doing her part to help get Kim and Colt married. Ally loved seeing Kim so happy, and Colt teased her constantly yet treated her like a queen. Kim deserved it, but Ally couldn't suppress an underlying pang that she'd never have that kind of future with Preston.

Preston had been out of it throughout the travel home. Gunner had let her stay by his side, and every time Preston came to, he would mumble about how incredible she was before passing out again. While she'd loved the sentiment, she was pretty sure it meant nothing. She couldn't delude herself into believing they'd built a lasting relationship in a few days in the alternate reality of the tropical paradise—and it *was* paradise even with the snakes, because she'd fallen in love with Preston there.

Carlos had destroyed her phone and she hadn't had time to go get a new one, but her dad had kindly retrieved her laptop and some things she needed from her downtown apartment. Every second she wasn't helping with the wedding or spending time with family, she was working furiously to catch up.

Bucky had told her not to worry about her social media campaign, but the season was fast approaching and she insisted they go for it as quickly as possible. She'd set up a press release for tomorrow morning, and she'd talked Mack Quinn and his wife, Sariah, into participating. It was the off-season and Mack and Sariah had a home in Golden, Colorado, but they were in Atlanta for Colt's wedding and had easily agreed to be involved with the campaign. Bucky had suggested they use all the speculation over her and Preston Steele disappearing to increase exposure, but she'd told him no, that was between her and Preston, and nobody needed to know what had happened but them. She was grateful Sutton Smith had made sure to keep everything quiet.

Her computer beeped with an incoming phone call from a

number she didn't recognize. The same number had called several times last night and again this morning. Telemarketers never gave up. She pushed a button to silence it and typed up some emails. She was all dolled up for the wedding in a pale pink gown with her hair in an updo. In only a few minutes, someone would come and demand she get powdered and perfect again. The wedding started in an hour, an early afternoon ceremony, and she'd been powdered and primped all day.

A text came through, and she was annoyed at the interruption of her scant work time, until she saw the words: *Ally, it's Preston ...*

A knock came at her door and she jumped, almost dropping her laptop. Her mom rushed in. "Hey, love. Are you ready?"

Ally closed the laptop, set it on her bed, and stood, smoothing her dress. "Yes."

"Working like always." Her mom came over and kissed her cheek. "That's my driven career woman."

Ally bit at the inside of her bottom lip. "Thanks, Mom." What else was she supposed to say? She was a driven workaholic, mostly because of the woman in front of her.

"Shar's going crazy making sure the caterers she approved of are going to have the food perfect for the wedding dinner, and Kim is going crazy because she hasn't kissed Colt in two hours." Her mom rolled her eyes, but she was smiling. "You girls keep life fun for me." Her eyes trailed over Ally. "You look ... lovely, dear." She almost seemed to force it out.

Ally's throat went dry. Her mother had never, ever complimented her on her looks. "Thanks, Mom. So do you."

Her mom waved her hand. "Pomp and circumstance. All that matters is who you are inside."

Ally stared at her mom. Of course what was on the inside mattered—but unfortunately, in this world, the outside made a difference also.

"Well, I'd better make sure your daddy is ready. Love you." She turned to go.

"Mom." Ally stopped her.

"Yes?" She pivoted.

"I know you think it's all 'pomp and circumstance,' but why didn't you ever tell me I was pretty?" The words rushed out and her cheeks heated up. She couldn't meet her mom's eyes. "I mean, I know I'm not a beauty like Kim or Shar, but ..." She took a breath and said bravely, "It's important for a girl to think she's at least attractive."

Her mom marched back and tilted Ally's chin up. Her eyes were kind but determined. "You are every bit as beautiful as Kim and Shar. I never wanted to focus on any of my daughters' exterior beauty. That's the world trying to make you settle for being a piece of meat, another pretty face."

Ally's breath came faster. "I understand you wanted us to excel for our brains and talent, but it is important in this world to feel good about yourself and know you're not ... revolting."

"You thought you were revolting?"

Ally nodded. "I thought I was chubby and unattractive and no man would ever want me."

Her mom's eyes widened and she groped for a nearby chair, leaning against the back of it. "Oh, love. None of that is true."

"Then why didn't you ever tell me I was pretty? Just once? Other girls heard it all the time; they were confident and knew they were appealing."

Her mom's mouth twisted. She looked at her hands for a few seconds and then said quietly, "Well, the truth is, it has nothing to do with you. You know your Aunt Nellie?"

"Yeah, she used to tell me I was 'big-boned.'"

"Oh!" Her mom's eyes widened and then narrowed. "How dare she? And behind my back, obviously."

"It's not like you counteracted it with compliments."

She nodded, accepting her responsibility in this just like she did everything, matter-of-factly. "If I would have known she said that to you, I would have ... Oh, it's pointless to talk about now. You know how obsessed she is with the way she looks? My parents never stopped telling her how gorgeous she was, dozens of times a day I heard it, and she became ... a narcissist who could never settle down to one man, always cheating and breaking hearts everywhere she went."

This was new information to Ally, except for the fact that Aunt Nellie was a piece of work. Yet there was a twinge of jealousy in her mom's voice. She'd felt like less because of *her* parents.

"So your daddy and I decided when we had you and Shar—and you were so exquisitely beautiful—that we wouldn't ever compliment you on your exterior beauty."

"I can ... understand your reasoning." Though she'd heard her mom compliment Kim on her beauty. Maybe they changed their plan with their youngest? Luckily Shar was confident enough that nothing could take her down. "Thanks for sharing that, Mom."

"I should've told you sooner. Maybe one or two compliments about exterior beauty would've been okay."

"You think?" Her mom had taken it to the other extreme, even gently redirecting others who said the girls were pretty, telling them about their accomplishments instead.

Her mom smiled grimly. "As a parent, you try your best and pray you don't mess up your children too horribly."

Ally didn't know what to say. It had messed her up, and the lingering feelings of being chubby as a young teen had never gone away either. "I know I was bigger as a teenager, so that was hard to deal with too as a young girl."

"But you've grown into your shape so perfectly." Her mom caught her in a tight hug. "You are incredibly beautiful, Ally, inside and out. I couldn't be more proud of you."

Ally hugged her back. "Thank you, Mom." She let it wash over her. She had grown past the chubby teenage stage, and though she had more curves than Beyoncé, Preston had been attracted to her. Preston! She had a text from him that she really wanted to read.

Her mom released her and hurried to the door, obviously done with the tender moment. "See you downstairs in a few minutes."

"Okay." Ally needed some time to process what she'd just been told. Her parents had deliberately not told her she was pretty, not because she wasn't, but because they thought it was best for her. It made sense and didn't feel like an excuse. Her mom was a good lady, but if Ally ever had children, she'd compliment them on their hard work, their talents, *and* their beauty.

It warranted further thought, but right now she needed to see what Preston had to say. Lifting her laptop open, she clicked on the messages. *Ally, it's Preston. I've been in the hospital, but I want to see you. Gunner finally got me a phone and your number. Can you call me?*

That was it. No indicators of how he felt at all, but he did want to see her. He wanted her to call him. She debated what to do, but she debated too long. There was a rap at her door and Shar pushed her way in, wearing an identical pale pink dress. It was going to be a great day with her family, but a long day of socializing. The last time she'd been at an event with her sisters, two different people had said they couldn't have told her and Shar apart, except that Ally was "curvier" than Shar. She hated to wish Kim's day away, but she really wanted to go see Preston.

"Help, sis! My zipper is stuck." Shar turned around.

Ally stood and worked the zipper up and down, tugging on the fabric that had been caught in it. Finally, it came free and she zipped Shar up.

Shar turned and hugged her. "Thanks! You look so pretty."

"You too."

"We've got to go. Mom's on a schedule." She winked and offered her arm. "After this wedding, I want to just sit and talk. I didn't get near enough details about the island and the beautiful man you spent plenty of hours alone with. There's a story there, I know it."

"I survived. The end."

Shar laughed. "You know I'll pry more out of you than that."

Ally smiled and took Shar's arm, giving one last longing look at her laptop. She hurried toward the door with her sister, though it was torture leaving Preston and that message un-responded to.

---

Preston's gaze darted around the spacious backyard, which looked like it'd been transformed into a flower garden. It was a large wedding party, and he just wanted the wedding over so he could talk to Ally. She hadn't appeared yet. He assumed she would walk down the aisle before the bride. It would take a lot of self-control to not interrupt the wedding by sweeping her off her feet and carrying her away somewhere private. He couldn't remember a lot of details of the island, but select memories kept appearing—mostly funny things Ally had said or done, how incredible it had felt to hold her close, and the overwhelming feeling that he cared deeply for her, but he'd messed it up somehow.

Music played, and Colt Quinn shifted nervously from foot to foot. His brothers were lined up with him, and Preston thought they were an impressive group of men. He really liked Mack Quinn, the huge offensive lineman for the Patriots. Mack was a true gentle giant.

Preston's eyes darted to the flower girl and the three women trailing down the aisle behind her: Navy Quinn, Shar Heathrow, and his Ally. Dressed in a fitted pale pink dress, Ally was incredibly gorgeous. Every soft curve was on display, and her smooth, tanned skin was just begging for him to touch it.

He started rising in his seat, but Gunner placed a hand on his arm. "Chill, dude, you can talk to her later."

Preston settled back down but had no clue how he was going to "chill". It had been two horribly long days since he'd seen her, touched her, talked to her. He needed Ally, and he needed her now.

Her gaze flickered to him. Their eyes met, and everyone else disappeared. She gave him a tentative smile, then focused back ahead as she walked with her sister until they stood next to the preacher. The wedding march started and everyone craned for a look at the bride. Everyone but Preston. He kept his eyes forward. There was only one woman he wanted to look at. She appeared to be watching her sister glide down the aisle, but then her eyes met his again. Preston's gaze didn't waver and he prayed that she'd know he was coming for her, and this time nobody was going to keep them apart.

# CHAPTER SIXTEEN

Ally could hardly stand still through the wedding. Preston was right there. Every time she so much as glanced Preston's way, he caught her gaze. He looked incredible in a navy blue tux, his dark eyes searing into her. What did he want, and why did he stare at her like she was his world? Their time together was a beautiful fantasy. It could never be her reality. He'd made that clear the last night in the tent when he'd turned away and asked her not to touch him.

She focused on her glowing sister and her handsome new husband as they kissed as a married couple, taking their own sweet time breaking apart. Colt swept Kim off her feet and carried her down the aisle, grinning as the wedding party laughed.

Shar hugged Ally and said, "Your turn next?"

"No, thanks. It's all you, sis."

"I don't know. Your story of the island had a lot of holes for me. Holes regarding the handsome man standing behind you right now." Shar winked. "Hello, Preston Steele."

Ally whirled and almost toppled off her heels. Preston offered his hand to Shar, but his focus was completely on Ally. "Nice to meet you, Shar Heathrow," he murmured.

"You as well. Be good to my twin sister. She's the best."

"I know that."

"You'd better." Shar nudged Ally with her elbow, then walked off to greet some close friends of the family.

Ally stood there gaping at Preston. He looked so good, and healthy. The last time she'd seen him, he'd been on a stretcher. "You're feeling okay?" she asked, clutching at her neck with her hand as if that could help her breathe easier.

"My head's okay," he said. He lowered his voice. "But every part of me has been missing you."

Ally's heart slammed against her chest. She wanted to throw herself into his arms. She laughed nervously instead. "I think that's just the brain injury talking."

"I don't think so." Preston's brow furrowed. "But I do have a lot of 'holes' in my memory."

She smiled at him quoting Shar. "What do you remember?"

"You being incredible—"

"You may have mentioned that a few hundred times on the plane ride home."

Preston lowered an eyebrow in confusion, then went on. "That's probably because the other things I remember are how funny, brave, and smart you are, and lots of kissing."

Ally flushed with heat. She wouldn't mind kissing him right now, even if the entire wedding party was watching. Which luckily they weren't, as all were focused on Kim and Colt. "You don't remember ..." She swallowed and forced it out. "Turning away from me the last night in the tent?" Why had she brought that up? Stupid, unconfident woman.

"I did?" But something in his voice said he knew that he didn't truly want her. "I made you feel bad?"

For a moment, she didn't react at all, hating that he was making her admit it. Eventually, she nodded.

"I have so many positive feelings when I think about you, when the memories of us laughing, teasing, or kissing come, but there's something uncomfortable too." He stepped closer and wrapped his hand around hers. "Ally, I'm so sorry that I made you uncomfortable. I don't know why I turned away. I'm an idiot. Please forgive me."

"But if you don't know why you turned away ..." Did he truly not? Who was she to question a traumatic head injury? But it felt like he should know. "Maybe you don't want to be with me anyway. Maybe you blocked that out because you felt bad about rejecting me."

"Ally." He shook his head and squeezed her hand. "Believe me— there is no world where I would reject you."

"But you did," she insisted, feeling petty and out of sorts. Why couldn't she just let this go and kiss him?

Two tall, leggy, gorgeous blondes sandwiched Preston between them and squealed. "Preston! You're alive!"

Preston's concentration on Ally broke momentarily. She made a break for it, not wanting to see him fawning over the women who were so similar to what he usually dated.

"Ally!" she heard him yell from behind her, but she kept on going. Hang the wedding dinner. She needed to escape. Kim would understand.

She made it to the back door when two hands grasped her waist and pulled her to a stop. She recognized the feel of those hands, and so she didn't turn around. "Let me go," she forced out.

Preston spun her around. "No. You have to give me a chance."

"Why?" She blinked up at him. He was too perfect, far too perfect for her. The talk with her mom earlier had cleared up some hurts for her and reassured her that she could be attractive, just like Preston had told her at their island, but she didn't know that she wanted to be with a man this beautiful, who women would always be chasing for his looks, his fame, and his talent. She didn't want the jealous feelings she'd just experienced to be a constant. It was at least another excuse to stay away from him.

"Because I've fallen for you, Ally Heathrow." She gasped, but he continued. "I don't remember what happened in that tent, why I'd turn away from the most beautiful and intriguing woman in the world to me, but I know what I want … I want all of you. Please give me a chance, Ally."

Ally studied him, not sure that she could just fall so easily. She was a strong, independent woman, and when Preston remembered why he'd turned away that night, he probably wouldn't want her anymore anyway. "I ... please give me some time."

Preston's grip on her waist slackened. "How much time?"

"I don't know. We went through something traumatic that bonded us together. You've had a bad head injury. I'm a mess emotionally. Please just give me a week, at least. If you still have strong feelings for me, then we'll talk." She knew her desire for him wouldn't change, but his for her could easily fade, especially as the two blondes were creeping up to them again.

"My feelings for you are just going to grow stronger," he insisted.

"We'll see." People were assembling for the wedding dinner on the tables across the lawn. "I'd better go sit with my family," she murmured.

"I'll let you go." Preston stared down at her, broodier than she'd ever seen him. "But I want you to remember something."

"What's that?"

He bent swiftly and kissed her. The pressure of his lips made her warm, tingly, and happier than she'd been since the last time he'd kissed her. His lips lingered over hers and he whispered roughly, "Remember that. I'll see you in a week."

Ally could hardly support her own weight as she stuttered away on her heels toward the family table up front. Remember that? She wouldn't forget that kiss or any of the others Preston had given her. She mostly wouldn't forget how much she loved to be with him or how special he made her feel. A week. A week was good. If Preston truly felt as strongly about her in a week, she'd propose on the spot.

# CHAPTER SEVENTEEN

Preston made it through the wedding dinner and the party, catching Ally's eye every chance he could and praying that she cared for him like he did for her. Yet he didn't approach her again, giving her the space she asked for. These feelings were new and tender, but they were overpowering. He wasn't going to let her go. How could he survive an entire week without her? He knew how bad the past two days had been. A week felt like a lifetime.

He chatted with Mack and Sariah Quinn for a while, and Mack told him they were doing the social media promotion for Ally in the morning. That stung. True, he'd rejected her idea back in Bucky's garden, but that had been before he'd known how incredible she was. Now he'd do any social media stunt she asked of him.

His family were still visiting him in Georgia from Boston, and they were waiting for him and Gunner to get back to Preston's home in Marietta that evening. The family ate a catered dinner at his mansion and talked late. Preston could see that Lottie was tipping sideways, she was so tired. He stood and scooped her off the couch. "Let's get you into bed, princess."

"You can't carry me; I'm too big," Lottie insisted.

Preston laughed. "Little girl like you? Don't insult my manliness." He remembered saying that to Ally. More memories of them teasing arose, but also of her admitting that she'd never felt attractive and thought she was big. He hoped Lottie never felt like that.

"I am big," Lottie insisted.

"You're all grown-up." Preston was realizing that in her mind, big meant old enough to be an adult.

She giggled and waved to the rest of the family. "Night!"

Everyone returned her farewell.

Preston carried her up the grand staircase to the bedroom he'd had all fixed up for her in pinks and whites. "You know how beautiful you are, right, sis?" he asked as he carried her into the room.

"Ah," she grunted. "Of course I do." As he settled her into bed, she clapped his face between her hands. "Tell me a story about you and love, bro."

Preston sat on the edge of her bed, and she released his face. "I don't have love, sweet girl. That's Slade and Mae."

Lottie looked at him much too perceptively. "You have love. I can see it. It's a sad kind of love, like *The Notebook*."

Preston didn't like that. In *The Notebook,* the couple was separated for years, and Nicholas Sparks's movies were just too sappy for him, not enough action or humor. Lottie loved every one of them. "It's not like *The Notebook*."

"Ha! You just admit you love someone."

"I don't love her ... but I like her a lot." Yet maybe he did love her. If only she'd let him stay close by her side, listening to her funny quips and getting to know her better.

"Who? Tell me story."

"Her name's Ally. She was with me on the island."

"I want to go there."

Preston chuckled. "I'll take you to an island, but not that one—the one we were on had snakes."

Lottie's eyes got big and she gasped. "I hate snakes!"

"Me too." He smiled. "And so does Ally. She let me hold her close when she was scared of the snakes." That memory, at least was vivid. Strong enough that he could feel her soft form in his arms.

"And you kiss her?" Lottie forgot about the snakes quickly.

"Yes," Preston admitted. "Multiple times."

"A long time?" She giggled.

"A long time," Preston said.

"Ooh-ee. You a bad boy, bro. Mama and Daddy say be careful not too much kissing."

"You'd better not be kissing boys," he said quickly.

"Not me. You! Too much kissing!"

Preston was overwhelmed by a rush of memories. Too much kissing. Kissing in the small tent. He'd kissed Ally passionately and hadn't wanted to stop. He'd gotten out of control, almost lost his head. He'd pushed Ally away and turned his back on her to try to keep from compromising her. *That* was what she'd been talking about. She'd said at the wedding that he'd pushed her away and he hadn't remembered it. She must not have understood he'd only reacted that way because she was irresistible to him and he respected her too much to be overly physical with her.

"Lottie." He hugged her tight. "I did kiss her too much, and I messed it all up."

Lottie pulled back and glared at him. "You better fix it."

Preston stood, intent on driving the twenty minutes to Ally's parents' home and finding her. "I will."

Lottie smiled. "Good night, best bro."

"Good night, sweet princess." Preston rushed from the room and into the great room area, where everyone was gathered. "I've got to run an errand," he said quickly.

"At eleven o'clock at night?" his mom asked.

Preston hurried to her side and bent down to kiss her cheek. "Yes. Don't wait up for me."

He ignored their speculative glances as he rushed through his kitchen area and into his garage. He jumped into his Lexus RC F, driving over the speed limit from his home in Marietta to her parents' house in Buckhead. This late at night there was thankfully no traffic, but the number on his dash kept ticking later and later. Would she be awake? He'd called her repeatedly last night and this morning and even texted her, but he'd gotten no response.

He finally arrived at the house after eleven-thirty. The house was dark. He didn't even know if Ally was here or at her own house. He knew so little about her, really. Did she even have a house, or did she live in an apartment? What was it like? He banged his head back against the headrest, not daring to go wake up her parents and have them dislike him before they even got to know him.

He pulled out his phone and sent her another text. *Ally, please call me. I know why I turned away that night, and I promise it has nothing to do with me not wanting you. Please. I just want to be with you.*

He sat there in front of her parents' house, waiting, but no response came.

# CHAPTER EIGHTEEN

Ally awoke late the next morning. She'd driven back to her apartment in the city after eleven last night and then had trouble falling asleep. Her mind had been full of thoughts of Preston and today's media event.

She rushed to get ready, excited and nervous for the press conference. She was going to present her idea to the world, with Mack and Sariah Quinn's help. They'd rehearsed it over FaceTime and it had gone fabulously. Everything was going to be amazing, if she didn't throw up. She selected a fitted navy blue and white floral dress, thinking she looked professional and feminine. She knew she'd never be thin, but Preston had helped her feel that her curves were appealing. To him, at least. Aw, Preston. A whole week until she found out if he truly wanted to spend more time with her, or if he'd already moved on to the next thin model. It felt like eternity.

Arriving at the Patriots' stadium, she took the elevator to the larger conference room, stopping in at the makeup and preparation room first. A crowd had already gathered when she was done there; the conference room was full of press and some Patriots' employees. Mack and Sariah were already there as well, and so was Bucky.

She rushed up to everyone. "Good morning."

Sweet Sariah gave her an impulsive hug. "You look beautiful."

"You too." Sariah did look beautiful in a flattering off-the-shoulder floral dress. She had scarring on her ear and neck from being burned as a child, but it only showed how confident and awesome she was that she didn't hide it. She looked miniscule next to her freight train of a husband. Ally wondered if she truly looked small next to Preston like that. She supposed she would. Preston wasn't as thick or tall as Mack Quinn's six-six and three hundred plus pounds, but he was still a big guy at six-four and two-thirty.

Bucky took her by the elbow and led her to the podium. He'd been very supportive of her ideas, and she didn't mind that he treated her like a favorite niece, not an employee. She appreciated that he wasn't using her and Preston's kidnapping to create more interest in the Patriots.

"You got this, girly." He grinned at her. "You're so gorgeous they won't even care what you say."

"Bucky, you can't talk like that." But she leaned in and squeezed him. "It's going to be great."

"I know it will. You thought of it."

The mics were all set up and the crowd quieted as Mack and Sariah stood up next to her. Ally said a prayer in her mind, straightened her shoulders, and plastered a smile on her face. Before getting to know Preston, she wouldn't have been confident enough to do this. She loved that he'd given her that gift.

"And we're live in three, two ..." The guy mouthed the one.

Ally was pretty certain she was going to throw up. She forced a grin and started talking through the plan: the social media blast, narrowing it down to a hundred touching stories, the voting, and front-row seats and a double date with Mack and Sariah as the prize. Everyone was smiling at her and Mack and Sariah were inserting cute quips. She thought it was going great, and she hadn't thrown up yet.

A reporter asked a question about which forms of social media could be used. Ally opened her mouth to answer, but the door at the rear of the room flung open. Preston strode in, carrying a shoebox and looking so incredibly handsome in a pin-striped black suit that she couldn't have remembered her sisters' names at the moment, let alone answered the reporter.

All heads swiveled, and a murmur of "Preston Steele" echoed throughout the room.

He confidently walked past the reporters and up front. His eyes were focused on Ally. Bucky backed away and gestured to Ally's side. Preston came right into her space and wrapped an arm around her. "I'm sorry," he murmured.

"For what?" she asked.

He grinned and looked out at the reporters. "Good morning, everyone."

"Mr. Steele," one of them called. "Are you here to support this project?"

"Yes, I am, and to support the incredible Ally Heathrow. Mack mentioned the press conference to me yesterday, and I thought, 'Now that's an idea I can get on board with.' So the winner will get the amazing seats Bucky's donated and have dinner with Mack and Sariah." He paused for emphasis. "The runner-up will get my front-row seats to the game of their choice, and have dinner with me and Miss Heathrow." Preston squeezed her waist. "That is, if Miss Heathrow approves."

Everyone's eyes swung to her. Ally was light-headed with happiness. Preston had come to support her idea. It meant the world to her. "Yes, of course. It's a brilliant plan."

Reporters started calling out questions, but Preston turned to her. "Ally, I'm so sorry. I couldn't remember everything, but last night it all came back. The reason I turned away from you was because you're the most desirable, beautiful woman I've ever touched. I turned away in that tent to preserve your innocence and virtue."

Ally's stomach pitched. Preston wanted her, and he wanted her so much he'd turned his back on her to keep her safe.

"Whoa, whoa, whoa." Bucky sprang in front of them and covered the mic with his palm. It was then that Ally registered how quiet the room had gotten. He glanced back at them. "Private conversation?"

Ally couldn't help but laugh. "You're teaching me about decorum now?"

He chuckled and uncovered the mic. "We're thrilled to have Preston Steele on board for this philanthropic mission. He and Miss Heathrow have some unfinished business from their time on a tropical island. I'll tell you a little about their crazy experience while they skedaddle to my office."

Ally gave him a pointed look.

He shrugged. "I'll keep it vague." He tilted his head. "Go!"

The reporters were clamoring for Preston and Ally to answer their questions, but Preston wrapped his arm around Ally's waist and escorted her out the rear door of the conference room, down a hallway and into Bucky's spacious office. Ally found she didn't much care what Bucky told the press.

Preston turned to face her and handed her the shoebox.

"What is this?" She opened it, and her jaw dropped. "My Christian Louboutins! How did you ...?" They were identical to the ones he'd chopped the heels off.

Preston grinned. "Sutton's men cleaned up the island, and Gunner was able to get a picture and the size of the shoes. Then, early this morning, Jex had one of his many girlfriends open her shop and get me the shoes."

"Thank you." She clutched the box to her chest.

Preston wrapped his arms around her waist. "Sorry, probably shouldn't have said that little bit about turning away to preserve your innocence on national television." He grimaced.

Ally set the shoebox on the nearby desk and reached up to cup his jaw with both her hands. "I don't care, as long as it's true. You honestly wanted me so bad, you turned away to stay under control?"

He nodded solemnly. "You're the only one I want, Ally, for your brain, your bravery, your sense of humor, your great attitude, but also your beautiful face and body. But I want to do this right, date and get to know each other."

She simply stared at him.

"Is that okay?" he asked.

"Is it okay? It's more than okay." She slid her arms around his neck, tugged him down, and kissed him.

Preston kissed her back, sighing against her mouth. "There are some rules, though."

"Rules? I don't like the sound of rules."

"Me neither." He pulled her closer. "But as irresistible as you are, I need rules."

Ally knew she'd never tire of him saying she was irresistible. Even more incredible, she believed him. "Such as?"

"No kissing lying down in a tent."

She laughed. "That should be easy, since I don't even own a tent. Do you?"

"No." He grinned, and he looked so good she could hardly resist kissing him again. "No kissing lying down anywhere."

"But kissing standing up in Bucky's office?"

"That I can get on board with." He lifted her off her feet and against his chest, taking his time exploring her mouth and lighting up her world. Ally didn't care where they kissed, as long as they kissed. She didn't care what they did for dates, or how long they dated. All that mattered was being with Preston.

# EPILOGUE

Preston and Ally were exploring the beaches of Tybee Island, near Savannah, with Lottie. Preston had the day off practice, and it was great to get away with his two favorite women on this beautiful fall day. They walked contentedly along as Lottie exclaimed over seashells and shrieked about jellyfish, stopping to chat with families on the beach and making friends everywhere she went.

"She's absolutely adorable," Ally whispered in Preston's ear.

"I only know of one woman who I love as much as her and my mom," he said back.

Ally's eyes widened and she stopped walking. They'd been dating for over a month now and he'd known he loved her since that day at the press conference, but he hadn't let it slip yet. He didn't want to rush things with Ally.

"Oh?" She lifted her eyebrows.

"Yeah. She's a beautiful, smart, funny marketing genius, who ropes me into all kinds of things I wouldn't normally do."

"Such as?"

"Jumping out of an airplane with Jex. Do you have any clue how many times I told him no before you asked?"

She grinned impishly. "I only asked once and you set it all up."

He nodded seriously. "I'd do anything for you."

"Such as?"

"You name it." He'd give her the world and it wouldn't be enough.

"Just love me," she whispered, looking vulnerable and scared as she said it. That girl was back—the uncertain girl he'd first fallen in love with on that island, who didn't know how desirable she was to him.

"I love you," he said firmly. "I love you," he repeated, louder.

"Kiss her, you tater tot." Lottie giggled from far too close, her face pressed up next to theirs.

They both laughed and Ally said, "He will, sweet girl, but first I need to tell him." She smiled sweetly and looked as innocent and perfect as she was, definitely not the driven marketing executive he'd once imagined. "I love you, Preston Steele."

Preston swooped her off her feet and into his arms. He kissed her until Lottie finally tugged them apart. It was just as well. Ally was simply too irresistible to him. He didn't want to rush things, but he was going to have a wedding ring on her finger soon. He leaned in close. "What do you think about eloping on a tropical island?"

She laughed. "As long as there aren't any snakes, I'm in."

Preston whooped and kissed her again.

# ABOUT THE AUTHOR

Cami is a part-time author, part-time exercise consultant, part-time housekeeper, full-time wife, and overtime mother of four adorable boys. Sleep and relaxation are fond memories. She's never been happier.

Sign up for Cami's newsletter to receive a free ebook copy of *The Resilient One: A Billionaire Bride Pact Romance* and information about new releases, discounts, and promotions here.

If you enjoyed *The Stranded Patriot,* read on for excerpts of Mack and Sariah and Mae and Slade's stories.

www.camichecketts.com
cami@camichecketts.com

# THE GENTLE PATRIOT

Mack Quinn, offensive lineman for the Georgia Patriots, followed the crowd of his teammates as they surged toward Hyde Metcalf, their wide receiver, to celebrate the winning touchdown pass. A win against Dallas on Christmas Day was great vindication after Dallas had beaten the Patriots out of their spot in the Super Bowl last year. Teammates slapped Hyde on the shoulder and someone hoisted their quarterback, Rigby "the Rocket" Breeland, into the air, but Hyde Metcalf dodged anyone trying to slow him down.

Staying close to his fellow linemen, Mack tried to keep up with Hyde, and blend in with the crowd. Not an easy feat when you were six-eight and over three hundred pounds. Luckily, Mack could move fast, even if his siblings and teammates teased him that he was built like a Mack truck.

He approached the sidelines and watched as Hyde launched himself over the barrier and into the waiting arms of his fiancée,

Lily Udy. Mack's gaze didn't linger on the couple kissing, he searched for the young woman who accompanied Hyde's mom and fiancée to every game. He stopped in his tracks and let out an audible sigh. Sariah Udy.

Somebody ran into him from behind, but he couldn't do more than mutter, "It's okay," to their apology. The woman of his dreams was less than ten feet away from him ... and she had absolutely no clue that he existed. Sariah was cheering, along with her family, as Hyde and Lily kissed and then Hyde started hugging everybody.

Mack had a great family of his own. He'd meet up with them after he showered. He'd bought them a private box last year when he started playing professionally. Usually, a few siblings and his parents were at each home game, sometimes the entire family would show. Today it was his parents, his sister, Navy, and his brother, Colt. Ryder had a game of his own with the Texas Titans tonight, Kaleb was doing a benefit concert in California for Christmas, and Griff was off saving the world somewhere.

He loved his family being here, but he thought it was pretty great that Hyde's family sat on the front row. Maybe he'd move his family's seats next year, if they wanted. The youngest in the family, Mack had never been one to ask much of anybody, especially his family who were much too good to him. He was blessed for sure. If only he could have the blessing of Sariah Udy noticing him. His gaze was still locked on her. She was helping Hyde's mom get her scarf on properly. It was a mild Georgia winter, but the older lady probably chilled easily.

Mack knew far too much about the Metcalf and Udy families. It couldn't really be considered stalking as they'd garnered a lot of media attention last spring when Hyde and Lily had a turbulent love story splashed all over the tabloids. Back then he'd found all the stories interesting about Lily's large family and how her six younger siblings had all fallen in love with Hyde. The first time Mack saw Lily's sister, Sariah, in person the stories went from interesting to fascinating.

Now, as he waited directly below Sariah, praying she'd glance his way, he started second-guessing himself. Just because he'd fallen hopelessly for her didn't mean she even knew who he was. Maybe all these times he thought she'd been tangling glances with him, she'd truly just been watching the game, or worse, she'd been staring at Tate Campbell or somebody like that who could flirt with a woman like her without their tongue swelling in their mouth.

Sariah finished helping Hyde's mom. The family was still focused on Hyde and Sariah's little brother, Josh, as he exclaimed over the game. Sariah's gaze traveled around the team slowly. Was she searching for him? Mack wanted to yell, "I'm here! Look down." But he didn't. He was the biggest chicken he knew.

Sariah finally seemed to sense him staring at her and her eyes met his. Mack tried to sputter out a hello, but he couldn't have said anything to save even his mama's life.

A slow grin curved Sariah's full lips and her deep brown eyes sparkled at him. She pulled her hair forward on the right side, twisting it in front of her neck. Mack was panting for air worse than when they made him run sprints at practice. He savored every second of the connection, knowing it couldn't last. He'd never gotten this close to her, but he'd watched her after every home game of the season. She'd head up the stairs with her sister and Hyde's mom soon and he'd be left watching her go, like always.

Instead of turning away she stepped right up to the railing, leaned over, and reached her hand down, still giving him that beautiful and inviting smile. Mack's heart leapt. He felt like a loyal knight who might get the opportunity to touch the beautiful princess' hand after winning the tournament.

Usually, Mack was light and fast on his feet, even with his large size. Right now, he lumbered forward, his size fourteen feet felt like blocks of cement, and all he wanted was to get close to her faster.

Finally, he reached the wall and luckily, he was tall enough he didn't have to reach up very far to wrap his hand around her delicate fingers. A zing of awareness and warmth shot through him. His brain tried to keep up with his heart but his heart was singing too loud, *Sariah Udy is holding my hand!*

She smiled down at him. The smile was sweet and welcoming and all the oxygen rushed out of Mack's body. He could face down the most vicious defenders on the field, but he had no clue how to react to holding Sariah's hand and having her smile at him like that.

The roaring crowd around them disappeared as they focused on each other. Mack knew right at that moment—he was in serious like and he had to do something about it. He'd dated different girls throughout high school, college, and the past couple of years women had chased him relentlessly, but he'd never felt a connection like this. This had to be the right woman for him.

"Hi," she said softly.

"Hi," Mack dumbly repeated. He squeezed her hand, he hoped gently, and searched his muddled brain for something poetic to say. His brother, Kaleb, was a professional country singer and had all manner of beautiful things to say or sing. His brother, Colt, was a professional woman-magnet and had trained Mack relentlessly on how to give a woman a smoldering look or say the right phrase to draw her in.

Mack prayed for inspiration and finally muttered, "Hi, pretty girl."

His face flamed red. What had he just said? He probably sounded like a creeper or something. That line had worked on his older brothers' girlfriends when Mack was eight and cute. Now he was twenty-five and hopefully there was nothing cute about him.

Sariah let out a soft chuckle and then tugged her hand free, waved quickly to him, and hurried to her family. Mack watched them all walk away. Her dad gave him a backwards, concerned glance, but Sariah didn't turn around or acknowledge him again.

Mack felt like he'd been slugged in the abdomen by his brother, Griff, the ex-navy SEAL who could take down any man. His big chance and he'd messed it all up. *Hi, pretty girl?* Sheesh, he was an idiot.

---

Find *The Gentle Patriot* here.

# HER DREAM DATE BOSS

Mae Delaney refastened her long, dark hair into its standard ponytail, pushed her large glasses firmly into place, smoothed down one of her favorite T-shirts, and made sure the screen angle didn't show she was in yoga pants at two p.m. She ran some pineapple lip gloss over her lips and practiced her smile in the mirror. "Look at you, you stinking hottie. You're going to slaughter him." The self-talk helped a tiny bit. She was the furthest thing from hot, and her thick glasses made it impossible to see her dark eyes, which her best friend, Kit, reassured her were her best feature.

Her stomach fluttering, she pushed the button on video chat to call Slade Steele: the most charming and handsome man on the planet, owner of Steele Wholesale Lending, and her boss.

Slade's perfectly sculpted face filled the screen, complemented by his deep brown eyes with lashes longer than her own and a trimmed beard that only served to highlight his intriguing lips.

He was gorgeous but so down-to-earth and kind. She scoured the internet nightly for Slade Steele sightings. Over the last few months, she'd seen him on humanitarian trips with his church, helping a child who'd lost his mom at a hockey game, taking his beautiful little sister who had Down syndrome to the premiere of a chick flick, and playing rugby with teenage boys at the park. In one of the rugby pictures, he'd had his shirt off. She sighed inadvertently.

"Hi, Mae. How are you today?"

"If I was any better, I'd be exalted already," she said.

He chuckled. "Well, lucky for me, you're still on this planet."

"Lucky, lucky you. Do you ever stop and thank the good Lord that you get the blessing of talking to me most days of the week?"

He grinned. "Yes, ma'am, I do." His eyes trailed over her T-shirt, and he read it out loud. "People in sleeping bags ... are the soft tacos of the bear world." Chuckling, he said, "Does that mean you have an aversion to tacos?"

"No, sir. I like tacos. I just don't want to be a taco."

He grinned. "Good to know."

All of Mae's nerves settled, replaced with a deep longing to track him down, throw herself against his well-formed chest, kiss him good and long, and tell him she'd loved him for almost two years now. Then maybe they could go for tacos. But thinking about his well-formed chest ... Could she touch it at their first meeting, or would that be an inappropriate action for a good Christian girl? She'd never really dated, so she had no idea. Hmm. It might be worth it. She might not get exalted as quickly, but she could repent later.

"Mae. Mae?"

"What? What just happened? Is it hot in here?" She fanned her face.

Slade laughed. "I'm not sure what your weather is like in Sausalito, so I have no idea. It's steamy hot in Boston."

Steamy hot? Oh, my. She wanted him to say those words again. Even better, maybe he could say them after they kissed the first time. *Focus, Mae.* "Dang man reminding me of the sad state of my life."

"What's that?"

"Never being where you are."

Slade's cheek twitched as if he was holding back laughter. "Can we get back to that state in a moment? I need some help from my best account rep."

"Of course you do. It's the only reason you ever call me." Of course he'd never call her for any reason but work. He was the perfect male model who dated the perfect female models. He lived in a different world than she did. At least she had these short conversations most days of the week, and she could dream of him.

"Must I remind you that you called me?" He winked, and Mae had to fan herself again.

"Stop flirting with me and tell me what the problem is."

Slade smiled, probably thinking he'd never flirt with the likes of her, but he was too classy to say that. He began listing for her which branches were having issues she needed to resolve. She was the liaison between his lending companies and the local mortgage companies. Mae typed away into her computer as he spoke.

"You know you could email me most of this?" Mae said, though she immediately regretted it.

"Don't say that. Then I would miss out on my daily dose of Mae humor."

"I'm actually funnier with my fingertips."

He blinked at her. "Hmm. Maybe I'll try email tomorrow."

"Please don't. I like seeing your handsome face." Her neck was burning, and she prayed that he wouldn't call her out or fire her for inappropriate talking in the workplace. But she worked remotely and he was the owner, so hopefully her blatant flirtations were okay.

"You're the one that suggested email."

"Forgive me. My brain vacates its lovely home when I stare into those deep brown eyes."

"Ah, Mae." He gifted her with his earth-moving smile. "You're good for the self-esteem. Hey, I've gotta run. I'm actually flying into San Francisco in a few hours. Do you want to get together for lunch or dinner tomorrow? I'll come across the bay to Sausalito."

Mae froze. Her stomach was swirling like it was full of butterflies, and her mouth and throat were so dry she couldn't even swallow. Slade Steele was coming to San Francisco, and he wanted to go to lunch or dinner with her?

*Oh my goodness! Oh my goodness!*

What should she do? Her brain whirled—play it cool, get a drink of water, find a firefighter to drench her with his hose, or call her sassy best friend Kit and have her come answer him? That would take too long, though, and he was staring at her, awaiting her answer. Mae tried to squeak out a yes, but nothing came out.

"Maybe not the best idea?" Slade asked, his dark eyes filling with concern.

If Mae missed this opportunity, Kit would sentence her to a year of walking lunges or some other exercise torture. Kit forced her to attend her boot camp class each morning, and it never got easier for Mae.

Slade waited, one perfect eyebrow arched up. "It's all right, Mae—"

"I'll go to dinner with you!" she yelled. "Yes!" Hallelujah. Praise every saintly ancestor she didn't even know and her beloved family watching from up above. She'd finally found her tongue and answered affirmatively, if a bit too eagerly.

———

Keep reading *Her Dream Date Boss* here.

# ALSO BY CAMI CHECKETTS

**Billionaire Boss Romance**

*Her Dream Date Boss*

*Her Prince Charming Boss*

**Quinn Family Romance**

*The Devoted Groom*

*The Conflicted Warrior*

*The Gentle Patriot*

*The Tough Warrior*

*Her Too-Perfect Boss*

*Her Forbidden Bodyguard*

**Hawk Brothers Romance**

*The Determined Groom*

*The Stealth Warrior*

*Her Billionaire Boss Fake Fiance*

*Risking it All*

**Navy Seal Romance**

*The Protective Warrior*

*The Captivating Warrior*

*The Stealth Warrior*

**Texas Titan Romance**

*The Fearless Groom*

**Echo Ridge Romance**

*Christmas Makeover*

*Last of the Gentlemen*

*My Best Man's Wedding*

*Change of Plans*

*Counterfeit Date*

**Snow Valley**

*Full Court Devotion: Christmas in Snow Valley*

*A Touch of Love: Summer in Snow Valley*

*Running from the Cowboy: Spring in Snow Valley*

*Light in Your Eyes: Winter in Snow Valley*

*Romancing the Singer: Return to Snow Valley*

*Fighting for Love: Return to Snow Valley*

**Other Books by Cami**

*The Loyal Patriot: Georgia Patriots Romance*

*Seeking Mr. Debonair: Jane Austen Pact*

*Seeking Mr. Dependable: Jane Austen Pact*

*Saving Sycamore Bay*

*How to Design Love*

*Oh, Come On, Be Faithful*

*Protect This*

*Blog This*

*Redeem This*

*The Broken Path*

*Dead Running*

Made in the USA
San Bernardino, CA
10 February 2020

64268487R00106